***Oh, heck, no,*** Lil dismay.

*Absolutely no getting* guy playing badass biker dude. Especially not a guy with the kind of look in his eyes that tempted women to sin.

He stepped into the room, abruptly dominating the space and sucking out all the air, replacing it with a much more potent cocktail of testosterone and pheromones. But then, he was a full-grown adult male who'd had years to perfect the recipe. *Oh, boy.*

His disturbing green gaze held hers for a couple of moments too long for comfort, and his mouth curled—as though he was picturing her in her underwear. *Jerk.*

Lilah felt her face heat and nervously licked her lips—which caused his eyes to heat instantly.

Couldn't he have waited for her to leave before arriving like a hot avenging angel of doom?

Dear Reader,

It's often said that our families are responsible for the people we become. If that's the case then I must be pretty awesome—because my family is the greatest. We may not always agree, but we never forget that blood far outweighs petty squabbles, and we're there for each other. *Always.*

My hero, Luke, isn't so lucky. He's grown up with emotionally unavailable parents concerned only with their shallow lives rather than being there for their three sons. And, having spent a decade in the military, he's more at ease with actions than emotions. Emotions are messy and they can't be trusted. Give him a crisis any day. He's barely survived his parents' marriages and is determined never to inflict that brand of marital hell on anyone—especially vulnerable kids. In fact, he's against marriage and children altogether.

But he does inspire trust in others. He's intelligent, a highly skilled soldier and medic, and he willingly puts himself on the line for others. If that's not hero-worthy, I don't know what is.

Lilah has a few "daddy issues" of her own, having experienced paternal rejection at a vulnerable age. She's bound and determined not to make the same mistakes as her mother. Fiercely independent, she would rather suppress her natural inclinations and go it alone than depend on someone who's not going to be there for the long haul.

Luckily for her, Luke is nothing like her father—or his. He's his own man, capable of making his own mistakes, and it takes history repeating itself—for Lilah, at least—to teach him that love begins with trust. And that, to my mind, is the true gift of family.

Happy reading,

*Lucy*

# TAMED BY HER
# ARMY DOC'S TOUCH

## Lucy Ryder

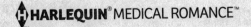

Recycling programs
for this product may
not exist in your area.

ISBN-13: 978-0-373-07016-9

Tamed by Her Army Doc's Touch

First North American Publication 2015

Copyright © 2015 by Bev Riley

Printed in U.S.A.

As always, I could not have done this without my amazing family, who are always there for me— especially my parents, Peter and Gillian Hucklesby. Mom and Dad, you're the best!

To my nephew Jason, who took time out of his busy study schedule to answer my endless medical questions. Thanks, Jay, you're going to make an awesome doctor.

And lastly, to my daughters, Kate and Ash. Words cannot express how much I love you.

# CHAPTER ONE

IF DR. LILAH MEREDITH had known she'd be
going swimming when she'd dressed earlier
that evening, she probably would have chosen
to wear something that didn't look like it came
from some designer lingerie's "wild" collection.

But then again, she'd recently returned from
the jungles of South America and had splurged
on expensive underwear to celebrate her return
to civilization. And if she was in an emotional
place where only she got to see the scraps of
silks and stretchy lace, then that was okay—she
was having a break from men anyway.

But that was before her evening, which had
started out normally enough for a bachelorette
party, had rapidly descended into disaster. One
minute she'd been surrounded by the debris left
over from the gift-opening frenzy, a tipsy bride-
to-be and a dozen giggling colleagues chant-
ing, "Take it off, take it off!", the next she'd
been scrambling through the open window be-

tween two ornamental shrubs onto the restaurant's upper deck.

She'd turned away from the embarrassing sight of a buff young guy stripping off his clothes to the bump-and-grind music blaring from the private room's speakers just in time to see a dozen people leap from the party boat into the lake.

Flashing back to her senior year in high school when a group of pot-smoking students had set fire to a boat, Lilah's heart stopped for a couple of beats.

Praying it was just another excuse for youthful high-jinks, she held her breath and waited for them to return to the boat. But the longer she watched the more uneasy she became, especially when it became apparent that someone was clearly in trouble.

With her heart surging into her throat, Lilah lurched to her feet and scrambled over the table to the window, knocking over half a bottle of Chianti and a jug of margaritas. Cutlery, glasses and flowers from the centerpiece went flying. There was a lot of high-pitched shrieking and Lilah had a brief glimpse of shocked expressions and open-mouthed gapes as she dived out the window.

Luke Sullivan folded his arms across his chest, tipped his chair back against the wooden railing and smiled as whoops and whistles of encouragement competed with the stripper music pumping from the system. Greg Turner, the man about to take the walk of insanity down the aisle, grinned goofily as Lindi—or was it Mindi?—ripped off her sparkly skin-tight blouse. She shimmied her balloon-shaped rack in the groom's face while her twin rubbed her awesome curves against him.

It wasn't that Luke had anything against stripper twins or lap dances—heck, he'd participated in enough as a wild student and then again in the army to appreciate the manly tradition. But at thirty-two, you'd think Greg would appreciate something a little less clichéd. Something like…poker night.

*Yeah*, Luke mused as the girl rolled her hips like a belly dancer. If he ever lost his mind long enough to get hitched—*God forbid*—he'd prefer poker night stag. Now, that was a civilized way to mourn the end of bachelorhood. *If* he were inclined to matrimony, that is, which he most definitely was not! He'd watched his parents' marriages fall apart too many times not to want to put himself or any kid through that kind of hell.

Besides, poker night was a great way for a bunch of guys to kick back, puff on Cuban cigars, guzzle beer and nachos, and talk trash as they bet on a pair of kings. He had a sneaky feeling Greg's wild younger brother had organized the strippers more for himself than the groom.

And while the twins were certainly impressively endowed, Luke thought with a yawn as his gaze slid to the people strolling along the boardwalk below, he preferred his women a little less surgically enhanced. And a lot more natural. Women were not meant to look like they carried alien pods on their chests. They were meant to be soft and curvy. Kind of like the woman dodging through the crowd, barely missing a collision with a couple of teens on skateboards. Her movements were urgent, as if she was either fleeing from someone or racing towards some*thing*.

Instantly alert, he pushed away from the wall and the chair legs hit the deck with a thud. He scanned the crowd for a knife-wielding pursuer but saw nothing suspicious and turned back in time to see her ditch her strappy sandals and hike the slinky dress up a pair of spectacular thighs, before taking off down the pier.

Grinning with masculine appreciation at the flash of long, smooth limbs, Luke rose and headed for the deck railing to get a better view. The woman slowed down enough to shout and wave her arms at the party cruise heading for open water. When no one responded, she shook her head and threw her arms up as if to say, "What now?"

Then, to his growing astonishment, she wriggled out of that short, snug dress—a sight way more erotic than the striptease going on behind him—and headed for the lake at a dead run.

Now, this, he thought as she launched herself off the pier, was way better than watching a couple of barely legal dancers prance around in strips of sparkly fabric. Her body entered the water with scarcely a splash, only to reappear seconds later as people began heading closer to watch the crazy woman take a swim in her underwear.

Just before the gathering crowd blocked his view, Luke saw her strike out, but not for the boat, as he'd expected. Instead, she headed away from it.

Puzzled, he scanned the water, stilling as he caught sight of movement a couple of hundred yards out. The person's flailing arms told him everything he needed to know.

Someone was in trouble.

Without further thought, he vaulted over the balcony and ignored the cries of surprise as he dropped to the boardwalk below. Wincing when pain shot through his recently healed thigh, he tucked in his body and rolled to his feet in one smooth move, before sprinting after her.

Barely a minute after the woman had entered

the lake; Luke was stripping off his own clothes and taking a running dive off the pier. He knew just how cold the water was and braced for the instant brain freeze.

Despite his training, he tensed as his body hit the water. *Jee-hose-phat.* It was freezing. After fifteen years as far away from the Pacific North West as he could get, the waters of Lake McKenzie still felt colder than the North Atlantic in midwinter.

He surfaced and sucked warm air into his lungs before setting out, his powerful strokes quickly eating up the distance. He was still a good forty yards away when he saw the woman disappear beneath the surface. A girl flailed nearby, alternately sobbing and screaming, "Trent! *Trent!*" as she tried to stay afloat.

She must have spotted Luke because her litany changed to, "Help him, help him! I couldn't hold on." She coughed and wiped her face with a shaking hand. "He…he j-just slipped under and I c-can't find him."

"Stay here," Luke ordered as he swam closer. "And calm down. Panicking won't help." He sucked in a quick breath and followed, his powerful kick immediately taking him several feet below the surface. As he descended, he searched for signs of the boy—and the woman.

Fortunately, light from the huge moon hanging over Lake McKenzie penetrated past the surface, eerily illuminating the cold, silent depths. Luke shuddered before he could help himself. He remembered quite vividly the summer his little brother had almost drowned in the lake and hoped, like that night twenty years ago, everyone walked away having learned a valuable lesson.

Luke looked for bubbles and when he caught sight of a silvery trail rising to the surface, he swam towards it just as a figure rose from the dark depths. It was the woman. She hadn't seen him yet and when he reached out to get her attention she jerked violently and turned.

Her eyes went huge and her mouth opened, as though he'd startled her. A couple of large bubbles escaped and a flash of panic crossed her features. She flailed then began kicking vigorously for the surface.

Realizing she'd swallowed lake water, Luke followed, grabbing her arm and pulling her upwards as he shot past. The moment their heads broke the surface, she slapped at his hands and fought for breath. Feeling a little guilty for scaring her, he grabbed her shoulders and demanded, "Are you trying to kill yourself?"

She made a feeble attempt to pull away but Luke tightened his grip and ignored the furious accusation in her huge eyes. She glared at him between violent coughing spells and he got the impression she'd like to deck him but was too busy hacking up a lung.

Finally she pushed at his shoulders and croaked, "That distinction's yours. Now let go." She shoved him again, and when he reluctantly released her she sucked in a jerky breath and pushed her hair from her face. Realizing she was about to dive, he grabbed her arm and got a foot on his thigh for his trouble.

"Wait, *dammit!*" he ground out, against the zinging pain that made his teeth hurt. "You wait here."

"No time," she snapped. "He's been under too long." And with a final yank she slipped free and he was left watching as her bottom and long legs disappeared beneath the surface.

Cursing stubborn independent women, Luke inhaled deeply and followed her into the cold depths. He'd been about to suggest that he take his turn looking. *Guess not.*

For someone already half-frozen, she moved with surprising speed through the water and he watched with reluctant admiration as long pale legs disappeared into the darkness. Unused to letting someone else act in an emergency, Luke used his big arms and legs to his advantage.

Finally, when his lungs began to burn and the need for air was forcing him to consider surfacing, Luke spotted movement to his left. Turning, he caught sight of a mermaid rising from the darkened depths. In the shifting silvery light her long curvy body and cloud of pale hair floating behind her reminded him of mystical creatures luring mortals to their watery doom.

Only this naiad was struggling sluggishly to save one. Streaking towards her, he wrapped an arm around the boy's chest, hooked his free hand beneath her armpit, and propelled them upwards with a few powerful kicks.

The instant they surfaced, her eyes met his in a long silent stare as she raggedly sucked in air. Before he could interpret her look or wonder at the weird flash of familiarity—or was it *déjà vu*?—she'd moved to support the exhausted girl. Luke was happy to let her go. He would rather take on a village of hostiles than deal with hysterical females.

He adjusted his hold on the boy and ordered, "Try to keep up," over his shoulder before striking out for the shore a couple of hundred yards away.

They needed to hurry. One glimpse of the kid's face told him Trent had suffered a head injury and was unresponsive. He only hoped the cold had slowed his vitals and they could revive him without permanent brain damage. The kid had been under at least ten minutes. Maybe longer.

He spotted a rubber dinghy speeding towards them and soon hands were reaching down to pull

Trent aboard. Luke was relieved to let them. The faster they began CPR and got the kid warmed up, the better.

He helped the coed aboard before placing both hands beneath the woman's scantily clad bottom and shoving her upwards. Finally, he hauled himself over the side just as the twin engines rumbled.

By the time they pulled up to the marina wharf a crowd had gathered. Several men rushed forward to lift their patient off the dinghy and Luke moved to help secure the boat.

The woman, looking cold but spectacular in a slinky leopard-print bra and teeny matching boy shorts, pushed past him and scrambled onto the pier, her low, smooth voice saying, "Stand back, I'm a doctor." She dropped to her knees and put her ear to the boy's chest before gently prising open his eyelids. Luke moved closer, urging the crowd back.

"Give us some room, folks," he said. "Anyone call 911?"

"On their way," someone replied, and shoved his clothing at him.

"Uh, thanks," Luke said absently, his attention already on the expert way the woman was performing CPR. He knelt down and faced her across the boy's prone body.

"Can you do mouth-to-mouth?" she asked, counting the compressions she executed.

"Hell no, lady," he said with a snort, and placed his hands over hers. "I'll do compressions. You breathe."

She slid her hands away and sat back, shoving ropes of sopping hair off her face. "Fine," she snapped, her expression annoyed. "But keep up a steady rhythm and stop when I tell you."

"Yes, ma'am," he said, his gaze dropping to her wide, lush mouth. "You just give that boy the kiss of life."

Lilah didn't know how long they worked on the unconscious student but she was grateful for the huge guy's assistance. He seemed to know what he was doing, like he'd done it before. She watched him correctly place his big hands and perform the exact number of compressions before pausing so she could inflate the boy's lungs.

The muscles in her arms and legs burned, quivering from the cold as much as from physical exertion. She was clearly out of shape. What made it worse was that the guy didn't even look fazed or out of breath. As though he regularly went swimming in freezing water to save drowning victims.

Maybe he did, she mused, absently noting wide, muscular shoulders, zero body fat and the impressive bulge of biceps as he crouched over her patient. But then again, it might have something to do with all that testosterone pumping off his big, hard body like a nuclear reactor. She could literally feel his heat reaching across the boy's body and wished she could borrow some of it.

He flashed her a concerned look, and Lilah knew what he was thinking. It didn't look good. She felt for a pulse just beneath their patient's jaw and thought she felt a tiny flutter. But when she moved her fingers slightly there was nothing.

She frowned and put her ear at his mouth. "I think I felt something," she murmured, searching for a pulse again.

"Keep breathing," the big guy ordered sharply, without breaking rhythm. "And don't stop until his pulse is steady and strong." Of course Lilah wasn't about to give up. She hadn't spent long minutes submerged in a cold, dark nightmare, thinking she was going to join Trent in a watery grave, to give up now.

They again fell into a grim, silent rhythm until she finally felt the tiniest muscle contraction beneath her hand. She reared back just as Trent's body jerked once, twice and then water began spewing from his lungs in huge spasmodic bursts. Applause and cheering broke the tense silence as she and her companion exchanged a brief glance of shared relief. Trent might not be out of the woods yet, but he was back.

Sucking in a deep breath, Lilah felt her body

sag. *Thank God*, she thought as the boy coughed and wheezed. That breathing—ragged and painful as it appeared—was the most beautiful sound in the world…as was the distant wail of sirens.

Pushing back the kid's wet hair to check his head wound, Lilah was unaware she was shaking until a large warm hand encased her trembling fingers. Instant heat and electricity shot up her arm, making her skin buzz. Startled, her gaze flew up and she got caught in eyes as deep and green and calm as the lake waters in summer.

Crinkles appeared at the corners and Lilah's heart gave a slow lazy tumble in her chest that she quickly blamed on the recent crisis.

"You did great," he said in a rough, dark bedroom voice. His darkened gaze dropped briefly to her mouth before lifting once more to lock with hers. His mouth kicked up at one corner. "It was obviously the kiss that did it. He's a lucky guy."

Feeling her face heat, Lilah slid her hand from his and focused her attention on examining the boy. "You just didn't want people to know you kissed a guy," she snorted softly and reached for a black T-shirt nearby, pressing it to the bleeding head wound. His deep chuckle vibrated the space between them and made her breath catch in her chest. Or maybe that was just because she was finally coming down off the adrenalin high.

"I can't imagine him liking it any more than I would." He was silent a moment before his large hand reached out to squeeze her shoulder. "Seriously, they're lucky you saw them."

Lilah stilled beneath his disturbing touch and his words. "Someone else would have helped." She looked up briefly as he rose. "You did."

"Couldn't let you have all the fun," he said, and something heavy dropped around her shoulders. Lilah was instantly enveloped in the warm, clean smell of virile man.

Without lifting her head, she snuggled into the garment and checked her patient's pupil reaction. "Do you know where you are?" she asked.

Trent opened his mouth and "Wha-a-at?" emerged on a ragged breath, as though his throat had been scraped raw.

"Stay still a moment," she said, gently soothing him when he made to sit up. "The paramedics are on their way."

He frowned and blinked. "Paramedics?" he rasped, his bewildered gaze clinging to hers, as though he was afraid she would vanish if he blinked.

"Do you know where you are?" she asked, just as someone cried, "Trent?" and the next thing the young coed was dropping down beside him. He turned to blink up at her for a couple of beats and Lilah held her breath. He croaked,

"Tiff?" and the girl fell against him, laughing and crying.

Lilah exhaled with noisy relief. If he remembered his girlfriend's name, his head injury wasn't too serious. She heard someone say the paramedics had arrived and rose to give the lovebirds a few moments of privacy. Within minutes Trent was being hooked up to a portable IV and loaded onto a stretcher.

"Is this really necessary?" he demanded weakly, as Lilah rattled off instructions to the ambulance crew.

"Yes," she said, giving his arm a reassuring squeeze. "But it should only be overnight. Depending on that head wound and the results of the CT scan."

"My head hurts." He frowned. "What happened?"

"You don't remember?" the big guy asked, as he appeared beside them.

Trent thought for a minute. "No. The last thing I remember was dancing with Tiff and then…and then people around us were jumping into the lake."

The rest of his answer was drowned out by the arrival of a group of tipsy women noisily pushing through the crowd. Before Lilah could question Trent further she was being enthusiastically hugged by her friends and peppered with demands about what had happened.

"You were with us one minute, the next you were flying out the window," Angie, a colleague from ER, laughed as she squeezed Lilah. "Heck, if we'd known you were planning a public strip-tease of your own, we'd have been there to cheer you on instead of that sleazy toy boy."

"And thank God you're wearing your good underwear," Jenna Richards, obstetrician and bride-to-be, added. "Imagine if you'd been prancing around in laundry-day undies?"

"Oh, horror," Angie gasped, and everyone laughed, clearly still buzzed from the evening's festivities.

Lilah pushed a hank of wet hair from her forehead and shoved first one arm then the other through the bomber jacket's sleeves. Now that the emergency was over, she was very conscious of the fact that she was practically naked beneath the butter-soft leather.

A cool breeze brushed her bare legs, raising an army of goose bumps and she burrowed deeper into the voluminous folds. She was freezing.

"Let's go," she said, pushing her way through the group, suddenly eager to get somewhere private—and maybe order a couple of brandies. For medicinal purposes, of course.

Sensing no one was following her, Lilah looked over her shoulder and found thirteen pairs of eyes studying her with an array of expressions varying from curiosity to narrow-eyed speculation.

"What?"

"Do you two know each other?" Jenna demanded, craning her neck to look through the crowd of bystanders.

Lilah frowned. "Who? Trent?"

There was general confusion but it was Angie who demanded, "Trent? Who's Trent?"

"The boy I—"

"We're talking about Lucky Luke," Jenna interrupted, gesturing wildly to the people crowding around the big guy whose gaze was locked on Lilah. Her breath caught beneath that intense gaze but she must have looked baffled because Jenna's mouth dropped open to a chorus of gasps.

"You don't know?" She looked shocked.

"Know what?"

"And the lucky girl just happened to see Dr. Hunk of the Decade in his skivvies," another voice drawled. "Did you know his father's a cyber-tech billionaire?"

Lilah followed the direction of the woman's predatory look. "Dr who?"

"Sullivan," Jenna prodded. "You know? The assistant director of medicine Sullivan?"

It was Lilah's turn to look shocked. "But… but…I thought the ADM was a…woman?"

"Honey," Angie said, her face lighting up with

a wicked grin, "Harriet Sullivan *is* a woman. You just got an up-close-and-personal view of her *nephew*, Dr. Tall, Dark and Buff, practically in the…well, the buff."

# CHAPTER TWO

LUKE CHECKED HIS side mirror, flicked on the indicator and turned his motorbike into the hospital visitors' parking. The sixteen-hundred cc engine rumbled beneath him like a large, hungry predator and responded to the merest flick of his wrist.

He'd been back in Spruce Ridge a few months and still couldn't believe he was here at all. But, then, Spruce Ridge had been the spawning grounds of the Sullivan boys' greatest summer adventures, despite—or maybe in spite of—their parents' widely publicized and bitter divorce.

His aunt and uncle had taken in three bewildered little boys and provided a firm hand and a ton of homemade cookies, along with unconditional love. Looking back, Luke sometimes wondered where he'd be if it hadn't been for summers spent here.

His mouth twisted into a self-deprecating grin as he recalled the wild scrapes he and his brothers had got into, partly in a bid for their parents' attention but mostly because they had been budding delinquents. And punishing his parents had been the main reason he'd joined the army after med school, instead of doing his residency at the hospital his mother pulled strings to get him into.

He'd loved every minute of being in the Rangers—right up until eight months ago when his helicopter had been shot down over enemy territory. The crash had taken the lives of six marines, two rangers, the hostage they'd been sent in to retrieve and Luke's passion for flying.

He and the rest of his team had held off hostiles for fourteen hours before help had finally arrived. Luke didn't remember the rescue. He'd woken up in hospital two days later feeling damn lucky to be alive. He'd also woken up realizing it was just a matter of time before his luck ran out, so he'd signed his release papers and hopped on the first flight home.

Locating an empty parking space near the entrance, he whipped the big motorbike between a faded red truck and a dark blue sedan and brought it to a halt.

Dropping one booted foot to the ground, he killed the engine, released the kickstand and rose to his full six-four height. Shoving up his visor, he stripped off thick leather gloves and turned to survey the parking lot in a move he recognized as a habit left over from a decade in the military. He wasn't concerned about being paranoid—it had saved his ass countless times over the years—but he still had to remind himself that Spruce Ridge wasn't a war zone.

He figured he'd eventually get better at remembering.

Reaching up, he tugged off his helmet and shoved a hand through his hair, ruffling the thick coffee-colored strands. After tucking his gloves in the helmet, he dropped everything into a side storage compartment then headed for the entrance.

People sent him wary glances and Luke smiled and shook his head as they scuttled out of his way. He knew the black leather made him appear the big badass biker, but he'd seen enough accidents involving motorbikes that he wouldn't consider getting on one without wearing all the proper gear.

Reaching for the big zipper tab, he pulled it down and thought about his favorite leather bomber jacket a certain siren had been wearing the last time he'd seen her.

The memory of huge stormy gray eyes framed by a thick fringe of dark lashes, long ropes of sopping red-gold hair and a lush pink mouth flashed into his head and brought a different smile to his lips. That mouth had breathed life back into a young man's lungs and had featured hotly in Luke's dreams last night.

Stepping through the automatic doors into the air-conditioned foyer, Luke pulled off his aviator shades and slid the earpiece of one arm into the neck of his T-shirt.

He gave a silent chuckle. Okay, so the memory had also included long naked legs and some spectacular curves covered in skimpy leopard-print underwear. He was a guy and hard-wired to recall stuff like that. Besides, in the months he'd been home he hadn't seen anything remotely as impressive or intriguing as the woman who'd stripped in public and dived into a freezing lake to save someone she didn't even know.

That had taken a lot of guts, and Luke was a great admirer of guts.

Entering the nearest elevator, he punched the button for the fifth floor and watched as the doors slid closed. It was his weekend off but he'd decided to check on last night's drowning victim before heading for the marina.

The elevator bell pinged and the doors opened onto a brightly lit corridor. Luke stepped out and the nurse on duty at the ward station looked up as he approached. Her gaze widened and she blinked a few times as her mouth opened and closed. "D-Dr. Sullivan?" she stuttered. "I didn't…I almost didn't recognize you." Then she hurriedly straightened her white and navy top and flipped her hair in a move Luke couldn't fail to recognize. "Can I help you?"

"I heard the drowning survivor was brought up here last night," he said, propping his elbow on the counter and aiming a crooked smile in her direction.

"I…um…drowning survivor?"

"Yeah, Trent something-or-another."

"Oh, him." She gave a husky laugh and slid her gaze all over him like he was a mega-sized chocolate snack and she was contemplating a sugar binge. "We heard all about his dramatic rescue this morning. Everyone's talking about what a hero you are."

"I didn't do anything," he denied, straightening from his slouch. He was used to attracting attention from the opposite sex, but felt like she'd stripped him naked right there beneath the bright fluorescents. He frowned. Sometimes he wondered if the interest had more to do with his father's money or the fact that he'd been discharged from the army with full military honors as well as a Purple Cross. Some women liked that kind of thing. "I wasn't the one who saved his life."

"That's not what I heard." She smiled as though he was being modest, and pointed down the corridor. "Just follow the noise. I'm sure Trent and his friends will be thrilled you stopped by."

"Thanks."

"Oh, by the way, Dr. Sullivan?" she called as

he headed down the corridor. "Have you seen the morning papers?"

He paused with a puzzled look over his shoulder. "No, why?"

She winked and fanned herself. "You really should check them out."

He shrugged and said, "Okay," although he had absolutely zero interest in the tabloids. He'd spent enough time as a kid trying to live down his mother's publicized exploits or dodging the paparazzi to care about reading whatever had the nurse looking like she was having a menopausal moment.

Approaching the noisy private room, he slowed his pace and came to an abrupt halt in the doorway. The private room was filled with young studs all vying for the attention of a woman propped beside the window. She was flushed and laughing, looking as young and carefree as a college sophomore. Luke recognized her instantly. Those long ropes of tousled red-gold curls were hard to miss, as were the soft, full curves beneath the lilac tank top. And the long legs encased in snug denim were unmistakably those of the woman who'd absconded with his favorite bomber jacket.

Dr. Lilah Meredith.

Lilah rolled her eyes and laughingly declined her fifth invitation for a date. It had been a long time since she'd been around noisy, energetic twenty-year-olds and she couldn't help feeling old—despite their assurances that she was a total "babe" or that she was only a few years older.

Besides, she couldn't remember the last time she'd been on a "real" date, let alone how to behave if she went on one with a couple of babe-crazy students.

Movement near the door distracted her from the disturbing image of herself as a lonely cougar—at twenty-nine—and Lilah sucked in a startled breath when she recognized the figure filling the doorway.

The last time she'd seen him he'd been standing head and shoulders above the crowd wearing nothing but low-slung jeans, a scowl and looking like the poster boy for Heroes R Us. The last time she'd seen him she'd thought he was just some hunky hot guy who'd been in the right place at the right time. Instead, he was a colleague—a guy from a world she wanted nothing to do with.

Granted, she'd only been working ER for a short while and had never actually been on rotation with him, but she'd heard enough about Luke Sullivan and seen him from a distance that she should have recognized him. But, then, she'd been too busy to pay attention to more than deep green eyes and big warm hands.

Now the sight of him dressed in black leather

and looking all big and bad and dangerous reminded her of long muscular legs, mile-wide
shoulders and a body made for underwear ads—
underwear for real men, that was, and not the
pretty boys they usually featured.

There'd been that brief glimpse of him last
night in wet black boxer briefs that still gave
her heart palpitations when she recalled the way
they'd molded to…well, everything.

Pushing away from the window with a breezy
"Well, boys, it's been fun," Lilah reached for
the shoulder bag she'd dropped on the bedside
cabinet.

She slung it over her shoulder to a chorus
of "You can't leave now," and pushed her way
through the wall of youthful testosterone.

"Since the real hero of the moment has arrived, why don't I leave you to introduce your-
selves? Maybe Connor can ask Dr. Sullivan for
a date. I hear he's—"

"Already got a date with you, Dr. Meredith,"
his deep voice interrupted smoothly, sending
goose bumps skittering across her flesh. Her
eyes widened. *Oh, heck, no*, she thought with a
gasp of dismay. *Absolutely no getting all worked
up over some rich guy playing a badass biker
dude*. Especially not a guy with the kind of look
in his eyes that tempted women to sin.

He stepped into the room, abruptly dominating the space and sucking out all the air with a

much more potent cocktail of testosterone and pheromones. But, then, he was a full-grown adult male who'd had years to perfect the recipe. *Oh, boy.*

His disturbing green gaze held hers for a couple of moments too long for comfort and his mouth curled—as though he was picturing her in her underwear. *Jerk.*

Lilah's face heated and she nervously licked her lips, which caused his eyes to darken instantly.

"Oh, I'm sure the guys will make much better dates than me," she said, cursing the alarming way her breath hitched and her knees wobbled as she moved towards the door. She paused and bit her lip when he made no move step aside. Her eyes narrowed. He was huge, *darn it*, and surrounded by masculine heat and energy that was way too appealing for comfort.

Couldn't he have waited for her to leave before arriving like a hot avenging angel of doom?

His hooded gaze swept over her face to her mouth before dropping to take in the rest of her body as though she was still wearing nothing but scraps of wet underwear. "I sincerely doubt that, *Doctor*," he drawled, drawing snickers from the group behind her. His mouth curled into a slow grin as sinful as the gaze that rose to hers. "I'll just keep my date with you."

"I wouldn't count on that, Dr. Sullivan," Lilah

said smoothly, and was forced to brush past his big body on her way out the door. A chorus of whistles and whoops followed her down the passage and she heard him say, "No offence, Connor."

A burst of laughter nearly drowned out Connor's reply. "None taken, dude," was followed by, "You lucky dog," before she was finally out of earshot.

Face burning, Lilah opted to take the stairs rather than the elevator to the ground floor. She hoped by the time she reached the lobby she could blame her pounding pulse and ragged breathing on jogging down five flights of stairs.

She hit the ground floor and moved across the huge foyer, nodding to a group of ER nurses, who grinned and exchanged knowing looks when they saw her.

Idly wondering what that was all about, she searched through her shoulder bag for her keys, looking up when someone called her name.

Two women who'd been at the bachelorette party the night before, approached. Kim Howard held aloft a folded daily newspaper. "Have you seen the tabloids?" Lilah frowned and shook her head wondering why she should be interested in the tabloids.

"You should take a look, girl," Mandy Morgan advised her. "They're calling you Wild Woman and speculating about which underwear house you're moonlighting for."

Lilah felt her mouth drop open. "Wha-what?"

Kim snapped open the newspaper and flipped it around so Lilah could see the headlines and color picture dominating the front page.

A loud buzzing noise filled Lilah's ears and she thought she might faint. Beneath the headline "Wild Woman to the Rescue" was a picture of her diving off the pier. If she hadn't been so horrified to see herself on the front page—in her underwear—she might have admired the almost perfect execution of the dive. As it was, her cheeks felt numb and her fingertips tingled as though she was about to pass out.

She grabbed the paper. "Oh, my God," she whimpered, too shocked to do anything but gape at the large color pic.

"There's more on page three." Kim bumped her shoulder sympathetically and Lilah turned the page with shaking hands. She gasped when she saw a grainy picture showing her stripping off her dress in full view of an entire waterfront packed with people. There were others too: of her stepping from the boat onto the pier; giving Trent what appeared to be a passionate kiss; and a close-up of her and Luke Sullivan sharing an eye-lock. The caption read *"Wild Woman and Dr. Oh-So-Dishy share a scorching hot look."*

*Yikes.*

She looked naked. She felt exposed and... and horrified. How could this happen? It was like she was back in high school and someone posted an embarrassing photograph of her on the bulletin board. Only *worse*. Because now everyone in Spruce Ridge could gawk at her in her underwear.

There was a pic of Luke in his wet boxer briefs looking buff and hunky. It was practically X-rated and Lilah could easily imagine thousands of women across the city drooling over him as they enjoyed their morning coffee.

"Where...?" She swallowed the hot lump of mortification that had settled in her throat and tried again. "Where the heck did these come from?" she rasped.

Kim's sideways glance was sympathetic. "Cellphones probably."

"Cellphones?" Lilah turned and gaped at her. "People were filming me with cellphones instead of doing something to help?" She knew she was getting a little hysterical and a lot outraged, but she felt outraged. "Two young people could have died while they whipped out their cellphones and caught it on video?"

Kim shrugged as if to say, *Yeah, go figure* and said, "Yay for teenagers and their technology. They must have made a fortune selling them to the tabloids."

Lilah's eyes dropped to the close-up of her and

Luke Sullivan and felt her face go hot. That simmering instant of connection had been caught
for all eternity by some pimply faced adolescent.
"This is a nightmare." Kim studied the picture
and Lilah felt the other woman's sideways look.
"What?"

"It looks kind of hot. Like a freeze-frame
from a movie where the romantic leads share a
sexy moment."

Lilah groaned and covered her face.

"It gets worse," Mandy said, and squeezed
Lilah's shoulder in silent support.

"How can anything be worse than this?"

"Easy," Kim said with a snicker. "You've gone
viral."

Luke approached the church and took the stone
stairs to the open wooden doors. A wedding
was the last place he wanted to be. He'd rather
be caught in hostile territory without a weapon.
But, last night, after he'd helped pour a wasted
Greg into a taxi, he'd made a solemn promise
that he'd be here.

He nodded to the guests gathered at the entrance and slipped his aviator shades into the inside pocket of his jacket. He'd had to buy a new
suit, but considering the last one he'd owned
was about nineteen years old he'd thought he
was probably due for a new one. Especially if
he was contemplating civilian life.

He might hate weddings and all they entailed but even he knew he couldn't arrive dressed in black leather. Other than a duffle bag full of army fatigues, jeans and tees, leather was all he had in his meager wardrobe. And owning one suit didn't mean he was turning out to be like his mother's husbands.

Resigning himself to a few hours of excruciating torture, he accepted a program from a pimply-faced usher in an ill-fitting suit and moved into the church, choosing a seat near the back. He'd come solo partly because he didn't know anyone outside of hospital personnel, and partly because women tended to get the kind of ideas at weddings that he wanted to avoid.

Besides, the only woman he'd been remotely attracted to since his arrival at SeaTac, just happened to think he was a card-carrying anarchist who couldn't be trusted. At least, that's what her expression had said this morning as she'd sashayed from a ward full of horny twenty-year-olds.

A low murmur of voices approached and a flash of ice-blue in his peripheral vision caught his attention. It was only when a tall curvy figure passed and moved further down the aisle that he realized it was the woman he'd just been thinking about. And she was being escorted by their boss, Dr. Peter Webster—smug ER director and all-round womanizing sleazebag.

Feeling his skull tighten, he watched as Webster indicated aisle seats a few rows down and slid in after her, moving until he was practically in her lap.

Luke narrowed his gaze and watched as Webster leaned close but with a quick head-shake Lilah Meredith shifted until there were a few inches between them. Were they involved or something?

And if he was asking himself what a married man was doing at a wedding without his wife, it was because he'd experienced first hand the devastation that kind of behavior left behind and not because the feeling in his gut felt very much like betrayal.

According to the grapevine, Webster had a habit of targeting young unmarried personnel and Luke wondered why no one had reported him. If there was one thing he hated more than a bully, it was someone using their position to sexually harass subordinates who needed their jobs.

And then he wondered why he cared that Lilah Meredith was involved with anyone. He didn't.

After the service he joined a group of colleagues outside and waited for the newlyweds to leave the church. And while everyone pelted Greg and Jenna with rose petals Luke stood with his jacket slung over his shoulder and his free hand shoved into his pocket. When Lilah finally appeared, Webster's proprietary hand was on the curve of her hip as he ushered her solicitously down the steps.

*Solicitous, my eye*, Luke snorted silently, and barely resisted the urge to head over and deck the smug bastard. He knew exactly what the man was thinking and it wasn't good manners— especially not with Dr. Meredith dressed in that blue dress and short stylish black jacket. All she needed was a wide-brimmed black hat and she'd look like a sexy gaucho.

Besides, it was none of his business how, and with whom, Lilah Meredith spent her free time. For all he knew, she was enjoying all the attention she was getting from a "respected" professional who could do a lot for her career.

Besides, when he'd been a student it had been common knowledge that a lot of girls dated med students, hoping to snag themselves a doctor. He hadn't thought Lilah Meredith was like that, but what the hell did he know?

Lilah drove through the huge iron gates and down the tree-lined road that led to the exclusive Greendale Hotel. Grimacing at the thought of how out of place her grandmother's old sedan would look amongst all the luxury vehicles, she headed for the portico entrance. She didn't know why she cared. It was way better than arriving in a low-slung sports car with a man who was not only her boss but reminded her of why her recent relief work in South America had gone so horribly wrong.

Peter Webster, with his charming smile, wandering hands and practiced seduction technique, was cut from the same cloth as her ex-boss, Dr. Brent Cunningham the Third—the person responsible for the Amazonian Disaster, as Lilah had come to think of that chapter in her life.

Like Brent, Peter suffered from a God complex and tended to think he was entitled to more than professional courtesy from his subordinates. As if Lilah should feel honored by his attention. She didn't, and had experienced first hand what happened when men like him felt rejected and humiliated by someone like her. Careers suffered and lives were ruined.

Lilah told herself to remember that the next time she felt like kneeing the man in the nuts or punching that perfect nose. If there was one thing she hated, it was influential men taking advantage of vulnerable young women.

Lilah was neither that young nor vulnerable, unless you counted on the fact that she really needed this job. Besides, every time she looked in a mirror she was reminded that her own mother had fallen for a man just like Peter. Handsome, charming, married and wealthy.

Rowan Franklin had swept her off her feet with promises of a bright and rosy future together. Only the future hadn't turned out so rosy for Grace Meredith. She'd found herself alone, pregnant and out of a job.

Frankly, no matter how handsome or charming the man, Lilah had absolutely no intention of making the same mistake—even at the promise of career advancement.

Following the stream of cars to the hotel's front entrance, she waited until a young uniformed valet approached her door before grabbing her clutch purse and sliding from behind the wheel.

She murmured her thanks and sent him a smile that made his ears turn red, before heading into the neo-classic lobby. A hundred feet overhead, late afternoon sunlight streamed in through the huge glass cupola and lit up the opulent marbled lobby like the sun god illuminating the temple of Zeus. Lilah had to blink a few times to dispel the image, especially when it highlighted a pair of broad shoulders, a wide tapering back and long muscular legs she recognized almost immediately—a figure that looked oddly out of place in the opulent surroundings when he should have looked right at home. Like a dangerous predator pretending to be housetrained.

She shivered at the image and decided it was

the coiled readiness and lazily alert gaze that took in everything around him.

As though sensing her scrutiny, Luke Sullivan turned his head and an errant ray of sunshine fell across his face. It illuminated a slashing cheekbone, hard jaw and a surprisingly sculpted mouth, leaving the rest of his face in deep shadow.

She watched his unsmiling mouth for a couple of beats and shivered again—this time for an altogether different reason. *Dammit*. The man just had to look at her and she was reacting like a high-school sophomore with her first crush.

Reminding herself that he was from a world so far removed from hers that he might as well be from another galaxy, Lilah bit her lip and followed other guests to the ballroom. She told herself that she didn't care since he was out of most women's league. But it didn't help.

It also didn't help that even in an elegant suit Luke Sullivan looked as relaxed as a warrior god in Zeus's temple—like a hero from the Golden Age. It didn't take much imagination to picture him swinging a huge bronze broadsword at some hapless mortal enemy or whipping out a handgun and going all Super Spy on hotel guests.

She'd seen him in scrubs and a lab coat, biker leather, formal suit and almost nothing at all, and had yet to decide which look suited him best.

He was a man of mystery, and Lilah didn't need anyone to tell her it would take a determined woman to peel away the layers to get to the real man beneath.

Not that he would allow it, she mused. The man had more layers than an onion and, frankly, anyone stupid enough to try deserved the tears that were sure to follow. She wasn't stupid and had long ago come to the conclusion that men weren't worth getting dehydrated for.

Shaking off the disturbing thoughts, Lilah paused at the ballroom entrance to scan the seating plan for her name. Besides, Luke Sullivan wasn't her problem and she would do well to stay as far from him as she could.

Someone come up behind her and she knew by the way her entire back heated and tingled who it was, even before a deep voice said near her ear, "Table eight, near the far left French doors. We're together."

*They were?*

Lilah turned and found her nose practically touching a crisp white shirt. Startled to find him so close, she took a step back and slid her gaze up past a green-and-gold-patterned tie, strong tanned throat and hard jaw. Her gaze lingered for a couple of seconds on his mouth before lifting to look into deep green eyes surrounded by fringes of long dark lashes.

Her stomach gave an alarming little dip.

"*Oh...uh...*Dr. Sullivan," she said lamely, and cursed the breathless quality of her voice. "It's you."

"Uh-huh." He lifted one eyebrow in a move that made Lilah wish she could look as mocking. "Expecting someone? Webster, maybe?"

"Peter?" Lilah was confused. "Why would I be waiting for him?"

Luke rocked back on his heels and shoved his hands in his pockets. "Peter?" he demanded with a ferocious scowl. "Since when are you on first-name terms with the Emperor of ER?"

"Since it's none of your business," she shot back, angered and confused by his confrontational attitude. The last time she'd seen him he'd been dressed like a bad biker dude. But at least he'd been smiling. Right now, glaring at her as though she'd done something unforgivable, he looked like a sophisticated angel of doom. A very *sexy* angel of doom. *Darn him. And darn those tingles.*

She turned back to pretend interest in the seating plan and tried to ignore the way the hair at the nape of her neck lifted—as though straining towards him—like he was a giant magnet yanking at every atom of iron in her body. Then he leaned closer and the tingles turned into a full-body shiver accompanied by goose bumps and tightening nipples.

Her eyes widened and she sucked in a shocked squeak.

*Stop that*, she ordered, but her body ignored the warning despite every instinct alerting her to danger. *Holy cow*, his blatant masculinity called to something deep and primal and feminine within her—something that had chosen now, of all times, to awaken and unfurl deep in her belly. She held her breath and kept her body as still as she could. Maybe he'd think she was a statue and go away.

*Please go away.*

"Why did you tell everyone I saved the kid, wild thing?" he murmured softly in her ear, and the breath she'd sucked in escaped in a soundless whoosh. She felt at once dizzy and amazingly clear-headed; something that was not only impossible but alarming.

And she didn't like it. And because she didn't, her spine stiffened and she said, "You did."

"Did not," he denied softly, chuckling when she made an annoyed sound in her throat.

Schooling her features, she turned slowly to face him. "I have no desire to become a celebrity," she informed him coolly. And she had no desire to become some rich playboy's newest toy either.

Luke rocked back on his heels, his hands shoved casually in his pockets. One dark brow arched arrogantly. "And you think I do?"

Lilah shrugged. "You have broad shoulders." She let her gaze drift over his wide, solid chest. "You can handle it," she added, before turning on her four-inch heels and escaping into the ballroom.

# CHAPTER THREE

THE INSTANT DINNER ENDED, Lilah escaped to the ladies' room to freshen her make-up and shore up her shaky composure. What the heck had Jenna been thinking to seat her beside Luke Sullivan?

Okay, so she knew what Jenna had been thinking. It was what everyone else had been thinking ever since the tabloids had hit the stands this morning. *Damn that picture.* And damn the rosy cloud of romance Jenna was floating around on. She was madly in love and wanted everyone else to be too.

Little did she know that Luke Sullivan was the last person Lilah would ever consider having a romantic *anything* with. And although he wasn't her boss, he was the boss's nephew. In Lilah's mind it was the same thing. It was a nightmare to go along with all the other nightmares she'd had recently. Like South America but with a guy she couldn't ignore no matter how much she tried. A guy who refused to *let* her ignore him.

The harder she tried the more perverse pleasure he seemed to take in sabotaging her. Like brushing against her when she talked to the man on her left or *accidentally* bumping her arm and spilling her champagne down her cleavage.

And he smelled delicious. Like warm, virile man and cool, earthy forest. Every breath she took filled her senses with his wonderfully warm woodsy smell until she was dizzy with the notion of finding out exactly where it originated. With her mouth.

Or maybe that was just the champagne.

Whatever it was, she became excruciatingly aware of his every move, and soon found herself holding her breath, waiting for his next. And, boy, he made plenty. Playing with the stem of his wine glass, invading her space while he kept her champagne glass filled, or removing his jacket and tie, rolling up his shirtsleeves to expose the corded strength of his forearms and his big boney wrists. Accidentally brushing his knuckles against her thigh.

And breathing. Especially breathing.

It all combined to make her as twitchy as a preschooler in Sunday Mass, and if she'd gulped down more champagne than usual, it was his fault. As was the headache blooming behind her eyes.

Exhaling with relief at finally being able to breathe without inhaling his potent masculinity, Lilah joined a host of other women at the mirrors. While listening to the gossip flowing around her, she spent a few minutes wrestling with her hair, even though she knew it was a lost cause. Taming the long curls had always been a challenge.

Finally, when she could no longer avoid the inevitable, she shoved everything back into her clutch bag and left the bathroom, praying Luke Sullivan had ridden off into the sunset on his big black hog. Maybe then she could start enjoying the evening.

Following the sounds of the band, she exchanged a few greetings with other guests on their way back to the ballroom and paused in the doorway as Jenna and Greg took to the floor for the newlyweds' dance.

It was a beautiful moment and she couldn't help feeling a little envious of the way Greg looked at his new bride. The couple practically glowed with happiness, reminding Lilah she hadn't had anything resembling a date in over two years.

The dance ended to hoots and cheers as the couple shared a heated embrace. Without pausing, the band segued into another song and the little pinch of envy became a sharp ache of emptiness as Jenna's father stepped onto the dance floor. He tapped Greg's shoulder then swept his daughter into his arms with a look of such pride and love that Lilah felt tears prick the backs of her eyes.

This was a moment she would never experience for herself. And though she tried to shove them back into hiding, all the old feelings of resentment and abandonment she hadn't felt since adolescence came rushing back.

Right there in the midst of celebration she was sucked back to her mother's death and the letter telling Lilah about her father.

It had taken her almost a year to get past the grief and anger following the plane crash that had killed her mother to summon the courage to open it. Sometimes Lilah wished she never had—wished she didn't know about her mother's summer internship at a prestigious Seattle law firm or her wild romance with the married son of the firm's founding partner. Life would have been so much simpler.

When twenty-two-year-old Grace Meredith had revealed she was pregnant, Rowan Franklin had been furious. He'd accused her of trying to ruin his life and his career, and then he'd offered her money.

Her mother hadn't exactly said it had been for a termination, but Lilah wasn't stupid. She could read between the lines. Even at sixteen she'd known her father had paid Grace to have an abortion then kicked her to the curb like an unwanted pet.

She clearly remembered hopping on an intercity bus with plans to confront him. Lilah snorted silently. She didn't know what she'd expected, but to a girl who'd dreamed of the day she would meet him, Rowan Franklin III had been handsome and dazzling as a movie star. She recalled being struck dumb in his presence as a chaotic mix of anger and desperate hope filled her.

Unfortunately, he'd been no happier to see her then than he'd been the day her mother had dropped the baby bombshell. He'd checked his watch and listened impatiently while she'd introduced herself and explained about her mother's death. When she'd finished, he'd walked to his desk, pulled out his checkbook, and without once looking in her direction he'd coldly asked how much it would take for her to go away.

She'd been devastated. With one stroke of his ten-thousand-dollar gold pen he'd destroyed a young girl's fragile dreams as easily as he'd signed his name.

So she'd reacted badly.

Lilah huffed out a silent laugh. Okay, badly was an understatement. She'd flung scathing insults in his smug, handsome face and when he'd looked her in the eye and denied being her father, she'd snatched some fancy glass paperweight along with several family photographs from his desk and hurled them at the wall of

glass cabinets behind him. The destruction
had been as satisfying as it had been horrify-
ing. Even to this day she couldn't believe what
she'd done.

White-faced with fury, he'd stalked over,
grabbed her arm in a bruising grip and dragged
her to the door. Then he'd slapped the check in
her hand and warned that if she ever contacted
him or tried to blackmail him again, he would
have her arrested.

She'd walked into that lavishly appointed corner office a nervous, eager child with dreams
of finding a father who'd been searching for his
daughter and had left with her heart and pride
in tatters. She'd also left determined never to let
anyone close enough to hurt her again.

That meeting had cured her of any "daddy"
issues she might have had. And just in case she
forgot, she'd kept that uncashed check of twenty-
five thousand dollars as a reminder that she had
to rely on herself and that some men made promises they never intended to keep.

Lost in the past, she didn't notice someone
come up behind her until a deep voice drawled,
"Don't tell me you buy into all this sappy stuff,
wild thing?"

Startled, Lilah sucked in a sharp breath and
rounded on him. "Will you stop sneaking up
on me?" she snapped, slapping a shaking hand
over her pounding heart. "And stop calling me

that." Besides, she didn't want to be anything like her mother.

Luke shoved his hands in his pockets and hiked a dark brow up his forehead as though she was acting crazy. Lilah felt a little crazy. *He* made her crazy, dammit.

"Lady, you're either in hearts-and-roses land or you need another glass of champagne." He snagged one from a passing waiter and shoved it at her. "Here, maybe this will help."

Lilah stepped back and looked at the glass like it might bite her. Frankly, the last thing she needed was another glass of champagne. Muttering something, she swung away to watch as other couples began drifting onto the dance floor. Maybe if she ignored him long enough he'd get the hint and go away.

But, of course, he didn't. That would be asking too much, Lilah thought furiously. Instead, he chuckled deep in his chest and leaned closer, the heat of his big body sending awareness shivering into every strand of DNA.

His deep voice held more than a hint of amusement when he asked, "Did you just say the only way champagne will help is if I drown in it, Dr. Meredith?"

Lilah fought the embarrassment heating her cheeks and inhaled slowly to give herself time to get a grip. But that only gave her a head full of his amazing scent. Besides, she hadn't meant for him to hear that. Had she?

She finally ground out, "Of course not," through clenched teeth and tried to edge away, but the darned man had practically herded her into a corner. She couldn't escape without drawing attention to herself, and after the past twenty four hours, attention was the last thing she wanted. "I would never be so rude."

He gave another chuckle as though he didn't believe her, and lifted his hand to play with the soft curls at her nape before drawing a light fingertip down her spine to the zipper tab. His touch, so deliberately casual, sent goose bumps fleeing across her flesh, and to Lilah's absolute horror, could be felt all the way to her tingling toes. Her belly clenched, her nipples tightened, and this time she didn't even have the benefit of her little jacket to hide her visceral response.

She hitched her shoulder to dislodge his touch and tried to move away but the man obviously had a hard head if he could ignore such obvious go-away signals. Instead, he dropped his hand to her hip and pulled her back against his chest.

She gasped and tried to jerk away but his fingers tightened. Heat instantly spread up to her nape and down to the backs of her knees—and, heck, everywhere in between. "What are you *doing*?" she demanded in a low voice, and tried to turn, but his palm slid across her jittering belly and pressed her against his front.

Lilah froze at the unexpected intimacy of his embrace. "You haven't answered my question," Luke reminded her against her ear, his thumb idly brushing warmed silk. His deep voice vibrated against her back like the rumble of distant thunder—or maybe a huge satisfied cat after eating a fat pigeon.

She sucked in a shivery breath and tried not to feel like a frightened pigeon. It was humiliating enough to discover how threatened she felt, especially when his touch heated up all the lonely places in her body that hadn't seen action in way too long.

"About what?" she rasped, her throat as dry as the Mojave Desert.

"About buying into all…this romantic garbage," he murmured, using his free hand to indicate the white-and-gold-decorated ballroom. Lilah tilted her head and looked up over her shoulder into his shadowed face.

"You don't?"

Amusement lit up his green eyes and lurked at the corners of his mouth. He snorted. "You're kidding, right?" And when she continued to stare at him he shrugged a heavily muscled shoulder. "I'm a guy. We're allergic to weddings." Her eyebrow rose up her forehead and he chuckled. "Okay, *I'm* allergic to weddings."

"Then why come?"

"I heard the food's great." He must have noticed her expression because he laughed and said, "I promised Greg I would."

When he laughed, golden flecks lit the green depths of his eyes. Like sunlight shining through water. "And you keep your promises?" she asked to distract herself from the feel of his hard body against hers and what it did to her.

Something indecipherable came and went in his expression and the golden lights winked out. "Don't you?"

"I asked first," Lilah countered, and instantly wondered at the shift in the energy around them. His eyes turned somber as they slid over her face before moving to the ballroom. She didn't know why but she got the odd impression he wasn't seeing the opulent room with its flickering candles and laughing guests. As though he'd withdrawn somewhere she couldn't follow— somewhere a lot less cheerful than a hotel ballroom in uptown Spruce Ridge.

His jaw flexed and she felt like she was intruding on a private moment filled with pain and bleak memories. "Some promises are impossible to keep," he murmured, and dropped his hand. Lilah shivered at the abrupt loss of heat and cursed herself for caring.

Something must have happened to put that haunted look on his face, she thought, fighting the urge to turn and wrap her arms around him. Luke Sullivan didn't need her concern. He was big and hard and capable. And dangerous. Very dangerous, she reminded herself. At least to her peace of mind. So when a young resident appeared beside them and asked her to dance, she accepted, suddenly eager to escape Luke Sullivan's disturbing presence.

She didn't know why she sent him a silent look over her shoulder. She certainly didn't need his permission. But when he shrugged and said, "I don't dance," before turning and disappearing from the ballroom, she couldn't help feeling rebuffed.

Fortunately the resident made it impossible to brood and before long Lilah was laughing at his bad jokes as he twirled her around the dance floor. Finally, after a dozen dances with as many new partners, she laughingly cried uncle and escaped out the French doors into the warm night.

A few people were scattered around the torch-dotted terrace and Lilah wandered over to the low stone balustrade. She looked out into a night as dark and lush as black velvet—a night perfect for romance and moonlit trysts. Frangipani and night-blooming camellia scented the balmy air while solar-powered lights led a rambling path through the extensive gardens to a pool, glowing like blue magic in the darkness. To her right the well-manicured lawns rolled towards the lake, slumbering like a sea of ink beneath a fat yellow moon.

The scene might have come right out of a movie if memories of the previous night hadn't flooded her mind. She shivered and rubbed her arms just as someone came up beside her. A jacket dropped around her shoulders in an echo of her thoughts but even before a smooth voice solicitously murmured, "You're cold," in her ear, she knew it wasn't the man she'd been thinking about.

Lilah bit back a grimace and looked up into Peter's handsome face. Just when she'd decided he'd lost interest, here she was cornered on the terrace in the dark. By her boss. *What joy.*

And from the look in his eyes she'd have to think of something fast if she wanted to escape with her job and her integrity intact. Something like an aneurysm or appendicitis. Or maybe mad cow disease. People tended to get a little paranoid when the words "mad" and "cow" weren't being used to describe a crazy woman at a Bloomingdale shoe sale. But then she reminded herself that he was a doctor and would know he'd have to eat her brains before contracting it. She couldn't see that happening in the next five seconds.

*Dammit.* She was trapped—by good manners and his hands on her shoulders.

"Finally," he murmured, like she'd been waiting all night to be alone with him. *Yeah, right*. In the moonlight his golden hair gleamed almost as brightly as his smile. Like an angel—or some equally perfect celestial being. And if she were any other woman she might have been charmed. But she wasn't. She had too much history with men like him to ever forget that he was married—and used vulnerable women.

"It's been torture, sitting alone," he said deeply, rubbing her arms, and for the second time that night Lilah felt herself pulled back against a man's warm chest. But whereas Luke's chest had felt wide and warm and oddly comforting, Peter's just felt…vaguely threatening.

"Miss me?"

And that was Lilah's cue to escape. She faked a shiver and seized the excuse to pull away. "I'm cold, maybe I should go in." His hands prevented her attempts to slide his jacket off her shoulders. They also kept her swathed in a cloud of expensive cologne and the cool calculation of a practiced seduction. Lilah shivered, this time it was genuine. She had an awful feeling the man had no intention of letting her go without a struggle.

Closing her eyes, she drew in a steadying breath and pushed memories of another man and another seduction attempt from her head. *Damn*. She really needed this job but Peter was making it increasingly difficult for her to remain polite when what she wanted to do was turn and knee him in the nuts and bolts.

Turning abruptly, she backed up against the balustrade and fought the urge to vault over it.

"Dr Webster," she said, deciding to confront him and risk being fired. "You're…um…my boss and…and married."

He hummed in his throat and stepped closer, dropping his hands onto the stone behind her, caging her with his arms and body. She had to press her hands against his chest and lean back to keep a few inches between them.

"My wife doesn't care," he explained with a smile, as though her protests amused him. *God, as though her protests aroused him.* "She does her thing and doesn't interfere with mine." He leaned forward to kiss her mouth but she turned her head at the last moment and his lips glanced off her cheekbone. "It suits us both."

"Well, it doesn't suit me," she said briskly, and grabbed his wandering hand before it could reach her breast.

He sighed and shifted back a little. "Don't tell me you're one of those women?" He sounded a bit annoyed, as though she was playing hard to get when she should be flattered by his attention. Lilah felt her jaw drop open.

"Excuse me?"

He must have heard something in her voice because he sighed and straightened. "All I'm saying is you've been sending out signals all night." *What?* "I'm not the only man to pick up on them, Lilah."

"Signals?"

His mouth slid into a charming, coaxing smile. "I am, however, the only man with enough balls to follow through."

Lilah stared at him as though he was speaking an alien dialect. Besides, the last subject she wanted to talk about was his...well, *that*. "What are you talking about?"

He sighed impatiently. "You're not making this easy, sweetheart."

*Sweetheart?* "Easy?"

"You're lucky I saw you slip away." She spluttered and he chuckled. "Let's not waste time," he cajoled gently, framing her face in his hands. "We can go back to your place, or get a room at the hotel if you prefer. Your choice. But you should know..." he paused and smiled meaningfully "...I can do things for your career."

Lilah stared up at him for a couple of beats and wondered if he'd lost his mind or was drunk. But he appeared sober and quite serious. As though she would actually consider taking him up on his less than flattering offer. She didn't know whether to laugh or slug him.

She shook her head and shifted to remove his jacket, but he covered her hands with his and drew the satin lapels together like a straitjacket.

Maybe he meant it to be comforting but she just felt claustrophobic.

"All right." He chuckled indulgently. "We'll do this your way. Why don't we go to the bar for a drink? Then…" He waggled his eyebrows and Lilah had to bite her lip to keep from rolling her eyes. She wanted to tell him what he could do with his drink—and anything else he was considering—but then again if she agreed, she could say she had to go to the bathroom and then make a break for it.

"Talk about what?"

"Yeah, Webster," a deep voice drawled from the inky shadows. It was so close that Lilah jolted and gave a little shocked gasp. She'd been so intent on escaping unscathed she hadn't noticed anyone approaching.

Luke materialized out of the dark looking big and dark and sinfully dangerous. "Talk about what?" he drawled, and Lilah wondered if she was the only one to detect the edge to his tone. His hair was rumpled as though he'd run his fingers through the thick strands. "About why you're moving in on my date?"

Looking at him, Lilah couldn't help comparing the two men: one as light as the other was dark. Both were tall and good looking, but where Peter was as smoothly handsome as a *male* model, Luke Sullivan was hot—with the kind of hard, dangerous edginess that made women stick out their chests and reach for lip gloss. He made her heart pound, her stomach clench and her knees wobble.

"Your date?" Webster laughed, as though the idea was ludicrous.

Luke instantly stilled and the air crackled with masculine aggression. "Yeah," he said mildly, his gaze on Lilah as though waiting for her to rat him out. "My date." She wasn't about to argue, even when he wrapped his long fingers around her wrist and slowly drew her towards him, making her feel like a fat juicy bone between two snarling alpha dogs.

Without looking at Webster, he slid the jacket off her shoulders and tossed it in the other man's direction. Smiling into her upturned face, he said, "Sorry I got waylaid, babe," in a voice as deep and intimate as a kiss. "A couple of the guys needed an impartial opinion." He finally looked up. "Thanks for keeping her company, Webster, but I've got this."

"You have?"

"Yeah." He leaned down and kissed Lilah's startled mouth and this time she didn't have time to turn away. But maybe that was a good thing? "The band's playing all those slow dances she promised me."

"Go away, Sullivan," Webster snapped, looking for a moment as though he contemplated wrestling Lilah away from Luke. "This is none of your business."

A dark brow hiked up Luke's forehead. "Not from where I'm standing," he drawled, lacing his long fingers with Lilah's and tugging her closer. She sucked in a sharp breath when the smile he aimed at the ER director turned blade-sharp. "By the way, where's that lovely wife of yours?" He looked out over the moonlit garden. "A shame to waste such a romantic setting."

Peter's gaze dropped to their linked hands and his mouth thinned. Lilah shivered and moved closer to Luke's comforting bulk. He gave her hand a reassuring—or was that a warning?—squeeze.

"Yeah," Peter said quietly, his eyes coolly speculative and not at all happy. "A real shame." And with one last look at Lilah he folded his jacket over his arm and walked off, leaving her alone with Luke.

As soon as he disappeared, Lilah slid her hand from Luke's and wrapped her arms around her middle. The whole incident had left a bad taste in her mouth and she was more than ready to escape the tension.

She moved across the terrace to the open French doors and Luke silently fell into step beside her. Sparing a quick glance across her shoulder, she had to tilt her head right back to see his expression. She should have saved herself the neck spasm. His features were shadowed and he was clearly back to his inscrutable self with his hard jaw and hooded gaze. The sight of a small muscle flexing in his jaw sent a brush of feminine warning drifting up her spine.

She swallowed hard and paused in the doorway to rub her tingling arms. "Where are you going?"

"We're going to dance."

"Dance?"

He spared her a hooded glance. "Yeah, dance. You know. I take you in my arms and we sway to music."

"I thought you couldn't dance."

Luke's mouth curled into a mocking smile. "I said I *don't* dance, not that I *can't*."

"There's a difference?"

"Sure." He snagged her hand and tightened his grip when she tried to snatch it back. "Why don't I show you?"

Lilah got the impression his suggestion was more along the lines of a command and suddenly she'd had enough.

"I don't want to dance," she announced stubbornly, digging her heels into the floor and trying to prise his fingers apart without causing a scene.

He simply ignored her puny efforts and growled, "That's too bad, wild thing," as he steered her towards the dance floor, where he yanked her against his chest and snaked his arms around her. They felt like bands of iron. "Besides, you don't want to make a liar out of me, do you?"

Lilah held her body stiffly and stared over his shoulder in stony silence. Perhaps if she ignored him he'd get bored and find someone else to torture.

After a short while he murmured, "I suggest you make it look good," in her ear.

Lilah tensed and sent him a brief glare out the corner of her eye. "Make what look good?" Despite her determination to remain unaffected, her body kept straining towards him, as though he was the sun and she a flower that had just survived a long cold winter.

Her resolve wavered and he must have sensed her indecision because his hold gentled and he shifted until her every soft curve was molded against hard masculine flesh.

"Webster is watching," he murmured against her ear. "No, don't look," he warned softly, when she began turning her head. "Unless you want him to come over here. Because if that's the case—"

"It's not," she said quickly, lifting her face to his. Her gaze drifted up his strong throat and shadowed jaw, past his sensual mouth to look deeply into his smoldering eyes. Lilah cursed the volatile effect he seemed to have on her senses—which were sending conflicting messages to escape *and* jump him.

Deciding to punish him for the way he made her body react—and for his arrogance—she allowed her hands to drift up his hard chest and over his heavily muscled shoulders. Then she thrust her fingers into the thick hair at the back of his head, her nails lightly scraping his skull.

His body shuddered—or maybe that was her—and with a rough sound in the back of his throat he dropped a hard kiss on her mouth. Unable to stop herself, she let out a soft moan and her eyes drifted closed. Her mouth softened beneath his and the rough sound in his throat became a growl of possession.

Right there on the dance floor of the Cherry Blossom ballroom, Luke Sullivan sucked out her mind along with her breath. The instant before her mind slid away completely Lilah reminded herself that it wasn't real. That the heat and hardness of him, the hungry feeding kiss that felt far too real, was all for one man's benefit.

And it wasn't the man currently kissing her like he wanted to consume her very soul.

# CHAPTER FOUR

IF LILAH'S INTENTION had been to get her life on track and keep a low profile when she'd returned to Spruce Ridge, she'd failed miserably. Not only had she managed to get herself on the front page of every local tabloid, the whole incident was also online—and, according to some colleagues, had already had a quarter-million hits.

And if that wasn't bad enough, she'd been hit on by her married boss, and a motorbike-riding dark angel with trouble tattooed on his sexy butt had practically sucked out her brains in the middle of a ballroom.

She was living every good girl's worst nightmare—and Lilah had made every effort as a child to be good so her mother hadn't had to worry.

And where the heck had that got her? She'd been fired from relief work in a developing country for challenging sexual harassment, photographed in public in her underwear, and caught on camera locking lips with a sexy biker dressed in an expensive suit at a society wedding.

The irony was not lost on Lilah. She'd spent her late teens and all of her adult life avoiding rich guys who thought women like her were easy pickings. Now she was being hounded by two of them while being accosted by the press and greeted everywhere she went as "Wild Woman."

She'd even tried hinting that Luke was a war hero to get the tabloids off her back but they kept coming back despite her refusal to cooperate. She sighed. Or maybe because of her refusal to cooperate. She didn't want the notoriety and the last thing she needed was for some reporter to start poking around in her life. There were things she didn't want people to know about her. Things more private than her preference in designer underwear.

Let Sullivan take the heat. Rumor had it he'd been a badass in the army. Frankly, she could believe it. He was surrounded by the kind of dangerous aura of a man who'd lived on the edge and liked it there. Besides, with his thick hide and military training, shouldn't he be fireproof?

Lilah might have wanted to forget the whole incident but newspapers were clearly at a loss for real news if they'd resorted to hounding her for a story that simply wasn't there. In addition, County Gen's director was ecstatic with all the free publicity the hospital was getting, and wanted to milk it. And if that wasn't bad enough, Trent's parents arrived from Europe the following week and Lilah received an invitation to dinner at an exclusive downtown hotel.

Fortunately she was on night shift and could send her apologies. She could understand their gratitude but she wanted to avoid any more attention.

Thinking she'd dodged that particular bullet, she arrived for work one evening to be informed that Dr. Webster wanted to see her.

Heart pounding in her throat, brow wrinkled with foreboding, Lilah made her way to his office and wondered if she was about to be fired—again. *Dammit*, just when she was starting to make friends and settle into the house her grandmother had left her.

Peter's assistant looked up as Lilah entered.

"Good evening, Dr. Meredith," Mercia Grant said coolly, slipping her purse strap over her shoulder and moving out from behind her desk. "You can go right in, he's waiting for you."

Lilah frowned. The last thing she wanted was to be alone with Webster—especially in his office during a shift change. No one was likely to notice if he decided to make good on his promise the night he'd cornered her on a shadowed terrace. Luke Sullivan had saved her then but she knew she couldn't count on that happening again.

Lilah said good-night and moved across the floor to the boss's inner sanctum with a jittery belly. She heard his voice and paused a moment before knocking. He barked out an order for her to enter and looked up when she pushed open the door. He was scowling at someone on the other end of the phone but when he saw Lilah his impatient expression vanished so fast she wondered if she'd imagined it.

He sent her a smile intended to flatter, as though the incident at Jenna's wedding had never happened. Gesturing for her to enter, he abruptly ended his call and rose to come around the large desk towards her—all congenial host— as though she'd simply dropped in for a social visit. *Really weird.*

"Take a seat, Lilah. Can I get you anything?" He'd recently showered and shaved and the scent of his expensive aftershave hung in the air. Confused and a little freaked out, she remained standing and shoved her hands into her lab-coat pockets.

"No, thank you," she said a little warily. "I have to report for duty in a few minutes and it looks like you're on your way to dinner."

"It can wait." He dismissed her objections, leaving her wondering if he meant her shift or his dinner. Sitting on the edge of his desk, he crossed his ankles and eyed her with an odd smile that sent a tremor of unease through her.

As though he knew something she didn't. "How are you, Lilah?"

Unease abruptly became confusion and she frowned. What the heck was he playing at? "I'm fine, thank you, Dr. Webster. The night administrator said you wanted to see me." *Might as well hurry things along so she could leave.*

He gave a low laugh and folded his arms over his chest. "I do. And I thought we'd agreed that you'd call me Peter?"

"You're my boss," she replied warily. *And you're a married jerk.* "Besides, we're at work."

He laughed again and straightened. "We are indeed." He headed for the coatrack near the window. "It seems that you have managed to impress quite a few important people," he announced cryptically, and Lilah didn't know if that was a good or bad thing.

"I'm not following you."

He retrieved his jacket and thrust his arms into the sleeves. "I understand the parents of the boy you saved invited you to dinner." It wasn't a question.

"I declined," she said, as he shrugged into the designer garment and paused before a large mirror to adjust his tie and fiddle with his already perfect hair. His gaze found hers in the mirror and she held it coolly and professionally. If he wanted to fire her, he would have to do it without all the schmoozing and creepy charm.

"Yes, well," he drawled, clearly amused by her attitude. "It seems our board of directors has decided to accept on your behalf."

*What?* "I'm on night rotation," she reminded him, relieved to have a legitimate excuse—and, *wow*, relieved that she wasn't being dismissed. Besides, Luke Sullivan had most likely also been invited and the last thing she wanted was to see him. Not after that very public lip-lock in the middle of the ballroom dance floor that had scrambled her brains. Not after he'd fried her nerve endings and sent her body into a meltdown she was still trying to recover from. All for nothing if the man she'd hoped to deceive was behaving as though that kiss had never happened.

Webster interrupted her thoughts. "I've ordered your schedule changed so you can have Friday night off," he said dismissively, turning to face her. And when she opened her mouth to argue, he added, "Orders from above. The Carringtons are insisting, and since they would like to thank the hospital by making a huge donation, the board of directors is also insisting."

Lilah frowned and firmed her jaw. She didn't like being outmaneuvered but didn't want to offend the big bosses either. On the bright side, at least she wasn't being fired.

Peter moved closer and before she realized his intention he'd lifted a hand to play with stray tendrils that had escaped her messy up-do.

"Why not think of it as part of the job?" he murmured soothingly, grazing her jaw with his fingers when she narrowed her gaze and stepped away. "Instead of dealing with the usual Friday night ER carnage, you'll have an excuse to wear something sexy and get to dine out in style. I know how much you women love that." Lilah's eyes widened. "Besides," he continued patronizingly, "I'll be there too. Maybe we can even make a night of it. A weekend perhaps?"

Lilah sucked in a shocked breath. *Was this guy for real?* "It appears that I have little choice in the matter, then," she murmured, with what she hoped was a regretful smile. "About dinner," she hastened to add, when she saw his smug satisfaction. "But I believe I already told you that I don't date married men."

His eyes twinkled. "Who said anything about dating?"

Lilah felt her mouth drop open. *Did women really take this guy seriously?* "I'm seeing someone else," she lied through gritted teeth.

He scoffed. "Sullivan?"

Lilah scarcely blinked as she again lied. "Yes." She was going to hell for all the fabrications popping out of her mouth. But considering it was for a good cause, she thought maybe God would understand.

"You're a beautiful, intelligent woman," he said, and Lilah fought the urge to roll her eyes.

"You can do so much better than a washed-up ex-soldier with no ambition beyond his motor-bike, the open road and wind in his hair."

She clenched her teeth to refrain from pointing out that he could hardly have wind in his hair if he was wearing a helmet. Instead, she shrugged and said, "He's single." Besides, Luke Sullivan didn't look washed up. He looked—okay never mind how he looked—but at least he wasn't using his position to get women out of their clothes.

He'd manage that effortlessly just by breathing.

Peter slid his hands into his pants pockets, looking all expensive and as shiny as a *male* model. She couldn't imagine him stripping to his tighty-whities and diving into a lake to save someone.

And why was she defending Luke to this creep, anyway?

"Is that what he told you?" He smirked. "Face it, what do you really know about him besides the fact that he owns black leather, drives a large noisy motorbike and can swim?"

*That he looks better in his underwear than most men look in expensive suits?* Okay, not a lot. But, then, she didn't have to. She had no intention of getting any more acquainted with either man.

She lifted her wrist to check her watch and frowned. *Damn*. Now she was late.

"I have to go," she said, turning to leave.

Peter followed her out his office and pulled the door closed behind him. "You know where to find me if you change your mind," he said, sliding his hand up her arm to cup her elbow as he escorted her from the outer office.

Lilah stiffened and sent him a baffled look when what she wanted to do was yank her arm away and yell at him to back the heck off. "I thought I'd been ordered to attend the dinner?"

He squeezed her arm. "You are." His voice deepened along with his seductive smile. "I was talking about the weekend."

She gave a mental eye roll and stepped away. *So not gonna happen, pal.* She aimed a regretful smile in his direction and said firmly, "I won't," before turning on her heel, feeling like she'd just dodged two bullets.

Luke pressed the transponder and waited for the SUV's alarm to engage before turning to head for the hotel's entrance. It was ten past eight and Aunt Harry had already called and texted three times demanding to know where he was.

He hadn't wanted to attend the damn dinner but Harriet had called, issuing a decree, and even though he'd reminded her that he didn't do fancy society dinners, she'd snorted and told him he should have thought about that before stripping to his skivvies in public to play hero.

There was something very wrong with her statement, Luke thought darkly. Firstly, he wasn't a hero. He just hadn't been able to stand back and let someone—a woman—put her life in danger to save a life. And, secondly, ever since he'd managed to get his half-naked ass in the newspaper, he'd been dodging reporters and fighting off women he didn't know.

Okay, maybe that hadn't been so bad, he thought with a smile, but he hadn't saved the boy's life. That honor went to the curvy redhead heading towards him at a fast clip, searching in one of those little purses that women liked to carry when they went out in the evening. A frown wrinkled the smooth skin of her forehead and her lush mouth looked sulky, as though she was annoyed about something.

He paused with one foot on the stone steps while imagining what she'd do if he pushed her up against the side of the building and took a greedy bite out of that soft sulky mouth— something he'd been thinking about ever since he'd kissed her at the wedding. A kiss he'd said was for Webster's benefit. He'd lied, and wasn't as ashamed to admit it as he should be. He'd wanted to kiss her more than he'd wanted to breathe and had used Webster as an excuse to taste those soft, lush pillows of flesh.

Hell, he'd do it again. In a heartbeat.

His mouth curved appreciatively as his gaze swept from the top of her shining head to the slinky four-inch heels on her slender feet. And instead of baggy scrubs or the lab coat he'd glimpsed her wearing all week, she looked like she'd been giftwrapped in black silk.

His eyes crinkled as he imagined unwrapping her to find out if she was sporting matching tiger-print undies. She liked people to think she was strictly professional, but Luke wasn't fooled. Beneath that calm competent exterior simmered a fiery passion that she kept on a very tight leash—as if she was afraid of what might happen if she let herself go.

Luke felt himself go hard at the thought of what would happen if and when she finally did.

He really wouldn't mind being the focus of all that wild passion. As Lilah had said the night of the wedding, his shoulders were broad—he could certainly take the heat. A smile tugged at the corners of his mouth and his mood rose along with his blood pressure at the sight of her long, shapely runner's legs. And since the evening had taken a turn for the better, he'd have to thank Harry for not taking no for an answer.

"Going somewhere?" he asked when Lilah was a couple of feet away. Her head jerked up and he watched her grey eyes go all wide and startled, like she hadn't expected him. Her lips parted on a silent gasp and Luke couldn't help noticing that they glistened with some kind of slick lip gloss he wouldn't mind eating off. He wondered if she'd taste sweet—like strawberries—or of something spicier…and darker. Suddenly he was ravenous.

She stilled when she saw him and her delicate brows pulled into a frown. "This is your fault," she accused, and his eyebrows rose up his forehead in surprise. Pressing his lips together to prevent a grin from forming, he shoved his hands in his pockets and studied her mutinous expression. She looked mad enough to slug someone. Most probably him, though he hadn't done anything. Yet.

"Oh, yeah?"

Her eyes snapped, turning the soft grey irises stormy. "I keep telling people you saved Trent and you keep telling them I did. And now I have to play nice with the big boys."

He gave her what he hoped was a wounded look and held up his hands, palms outwards. "Hey, don't look at me. I don't want to be here any more than you do."

Her snort told him what she thought of his excuse but when she lifted a hand to adjust a sparkly earring he noticed it was shaking. "Hey." He caught her cold fingers, his study of her face revealing pale flawless skin and smoky eyes

dark with distress. She was trembling and trying not to let it show.

"What happened?"

She said "Nothing," and tried to snatch her
hand back.

But Luke tightened his grip and repeated,
"What happened?"

A host of emotions flashed across her face
and she visibly tried to pull herself together by
inhaling. If Luke hadn't been so concerned, he
might have suffered an instant aneurysm when
the tops of her creamy breasts rose above the
fitted bodice. Fortunately he'd been trained not
to allow distractions to…well, distract him. It's
what got a guy killed. *Or led to disaster.*

"Some idiot nearly ran me off the road," she
admitted grudgingly, and he forgot all about full
creamy breasts and big grey eyes. Okay, maybe
not *forgot*, but he was instantly alert and able to
focus all his attention on the conversation.

"Where?" he demanded, moving to shield
her body with his as his eyes scanned the busy
street. "What kind of car was he driving? Did
you get the registration? Are you all right?"

Lilah's mouth curved into a reluctant smile
and the tightness around her eyes eased a frac-
tion. "Just before Bretton Bridge, a dark sedan,
no, it happened too fast, and, yes, I'm fine—just
a little shook up."

He rubbed his thumb across the silky skin of

her wrist, hoping to soothe her wildly fluttering pulse. When faint color flooded her cheeks, he smiled down at her. "There, that's better. But, seriously, are you sure you don't need a drink first? We can always duck into the bar and hope no one notices that we're missing."

She gave a low husky laugh that he felt all the way to his gut, which tightened almost painfully in reaction. Releasing her hand, he slid his palm to the curve of her waist, the need to touch any part of her overwhelming his good sense.

"I'm fine, really," she said to his chin, as he escorted her into the lobby. "Besides, it's late and everyone will be wondering where we are."

Luke scowled. "By everyone, you mean Webster?" he growled, with something that felt very much like possessiveness tightening his mouth.

She paused to frown over her shoulder and he pointedly ignored the expression on her face that said he was crazy. Hell, he felt a little crazy.

"No, I don't mean him," she snapped irritably. "I'm talking about our bosses, the hospital directors. I don't even know if Webster will be there. And while we're on the subject, I guess you should know I may have hinted that we were…are…um, involved." The last emerged on a breathless rush.

Luke stilled in the process of punching the call button for the fourth time and turned to stare at her. "We as in…?"

Lilah flushed and her gaze skittered away from his. Her tongue emerged to moisten her lips and Luke grinned, his good mood abruptly restored.

Arching his brow, he waved a hand between them. "We? As in you and…me?"

Her flush deepened and she fiddled with her purse. "It's your fault," she snapped. "If you hadn't…um, kissed me on the…um…dance floor, none of this would be necessary."

The doors slid open and Luke ushered her into the elevator, punching the number for the roof restaurant. "And by necessary, you mean what exactly?" he drawled, and when she nibbled nervously on her lip Luke finally understood. The guy was harassing her again. "Why don't you just report him to Personnel?"

Lilah rolled her eyes. "The last person to do that was fired."

"What do you mean, fired?" he demanded in a way that had Lilah staring at him, like he was being deliberately obtuse.

"A lowly nurse accuses a prominent doctor of sexual harassment? Who do you think people are going to believe?" She snorted inelegantly and glared at him as though he was to blame for the inequality as well as the harassment. "Who do people usually believe? The man, that's who, especially when he's rich and powerful."

Luke grunted, silently admitting that she was

right, except for one thing. The only thing prominent about Webster was his monumental ego.

Folding his arms across his chest, he propped his shoulder against the elevator wall. "So…how involved are we? Casually or…uh, intimately?"

Lilah's strangled growl made him want to laugh. Schooling his features, he shrugged. "I'm only asking so I know exactly how I'm supposed to act," he explained, sweeping his gaze over her. "You know."

She stared up at him and swallowed hard as the light for the third floor blinked on and then off. "Know what?"

"Well…look at you," he said, waving his hand vaguely in her direction.

Her spine snapped straight. "What's…wrong with me?" she demanded, sounding so offended that Luke's mouth curled despite his attempts to appear indifferent.

"You look too uptight to be involved with me."

Lilah's eyes narrowed. "Too…uptight?"

He tilted his head to the side and scratched his chin as though considering her appearance. "It's the hair." She sputtered for a couple of beats and lifted a hand to her head as if to make sure it was still ruthlessly pulled back into a professional bun.

"What's wrong with my hair?"

He gave an apologetic shrug and lied. "You look like a librarian." She didn't look anything like a librarian. Not with those thunderous grey eyes glaring holes in him, and certainly not with all those curves shrink-wrapped in black silk like a decadent seal-a-meal.

He affected a casual shrug and pursed his lips to keep from laughing at her murderous expression. "If you want Webster to believe we're... what was the word you used?" He arched his brow. "Involved? Then you have to let me make a few modifications."

Her mouth dropped open. "Mo-modifications?"

"Yeah, and we'd better hurry," he said, tugging her closer. "These hi-tech elevators are fast." And before she could demand what the heck he thought he was doing, Luke reached up and plucked the pins holding the mass of hair at the nape of her neck.

"What are you *doing*?" Lilah shrieked, slapping at his hands to keep her French twist from unravelling, but Luke thrust his fingers into her thick hair and with a few deft moves the long curly ropes fell around her shoulders in a glorious cloud of sunset-colored silk.

"*Dammit*, Sullivan," she growled furiously, shoving at his hands. "Now I look like I just crawled out of bed."

Luke's gaze slid over her beautiful face, all flushed with annoyance, and landed on her sulky mouth.

"Not yet you don't," he murmured, and jerked her against him. She squeaked and he took full advantage of her surprise to cover her mouth with his in a kiss that instantly caught fire and shattered his composure. He went from semi to hard in an instant and it was a struggle to keep his hands cupped around her head.

Not that she was trying to escape, Luke thought with fierce satisfaction as the rigid lines of her body softened gradually until she was plastered up against him like a spray tan.

Her breath hitched in her throat and with a rough growl he backed her against the wall and did what he'd thought about earlier. He planted his hands beside her head and fed her hot, demanding kisses as he ate the lip gloss off her mouth. He knew if he touched all that soft, silky flesh he might forget where they were.

He didn't slide into the kiss like he wanted to. There wasn't time. Besides, her mouth softened and clung. *God*…she tasted so good that he was devouring her before he could think that maybe this was a bad idea. A very, very bad idea.

# CHAPTER FIVE

THE ELEVATOR RAIL dug into Lilah's back as Luke pressed her into the wall, his body all hot and hard and impatient against hers. She'd had a split second to react before his mouth closed over hers and he was devouring her like he hadn't eaten in a year. She might have put up a token protest if the air around them hadn't instantly turned to steam or if her deprived body hadn't strained towards his—completely without her consent, of course.

And, boy, was she glad his body was plastered all over the front of hers, especially as she couldn't feel her legs and was certain she would slide to the floor without him.

His tongue stroked hers and his mouth created a light suction that almost had her hair catching fire like she'd been plugged into a three-phase transformer. She would have gasped if he hadn't stolen her breath along with her mind.

Dizzy, Lilah curled her hands into his pristine shirtfront and surrendered to the consuming heat of his kiss. She wanted to touch him. She wanted him to touch her—all over—but all he did was touch her with his mouth and feed her wild, hungry kisses while devouring her good sense.

He growled low in his throat as he abandoned her mouth to drag his lips along her jaw. He licked at the delicate skin of her throat and closed his teeth on the tendon joining her neck and shoulder, sending sensation shooting through her body like a hot bolt of lightning.

Lilah shuddered, half expecting her head to explode. Her belly clenched and searing heat rolled over her as everything beneath her sensitive flesh turned liquid.

And then his tongue drew a line of fire down the wide bodice of her dress to where her breasts rose and fell with choppy breaths. She moaned, moving restlessly against him and nearly combusted when the long, thick ridge of his arousal pressed against her. Right where a painful, empty ache blossomed.

"*Stop*," she gasped, and thrust her hands into his hair, unsure whether to hold onto him or push him the heck away. Her nails scraped along his scalp and his big body shuddered against her.

Or was that her?

With a low, savage growl he opened his lips on the exposed upper curve of her breast and drew the soft flesh into the hot, wet cavern of his mouth. Any thought she might have had to push him away vaporized. Her head went light, her body shuddered and for one awful, wonderful moment Lilah thought she might actually faint or…or…

A low, husky whimper escaped and lights exploded behind her eyelids. Someone cleared their throat, followed by muffled chuckles, forcing Lilah to frown and lift oddly heavy lashes at the unwelcome intrusion. And when the haze cleared, her horrified gaze encountered the amused faces of almost a dozen people watching her make a spectacle of herself.

With a squeak of horror Lilah straightened like she'd been shot. Several more flashes blinded her and she shoved frantically at Luke's big shoulders when what she really wanted to do was to bury her flaming face in his chest and pretend she hadn't just been photographed having her…um…chest sucked.

*Oh, boy.* They'd been caught making out in an elevator like a couple of randy adolescents. By their bosses.

For one scorching instant his hot, sleepy gaze caught and held hers before he drew in a deep breath and then expelled it in a noisy whoosh. Like he'd been floored.

*God, she knew the feeling.*

Finally Luke turned and aimed a crooked grin

at their smiling audience, as though he regularly got caught in elevators kissing women senseless.

He probably did, Lilah thought darkly, ducking behind his bulk to hastily tug her bodice and hem into place. She sucked in a shaky breath and smoothed the messy tangle of curls off her face, praying she didn't look like she'd been dragged through a hedge backwards—or have a man ravish her within an inch of her sanity.

And from the satisfied gleam in Luke's green eyes it was the latter. And exactly what he'd intended.

"Sorry we're late," he drawled, bending to retrieve the purse Lilah couldn't recall dropping. He handed it to her, and with warm fingers wrapped around her arm, ushered her from the elevator as though he knew her knees were wobbly—or maybe suspected that she wanted to bolt. "We were...unaccountably delayed."

Everyone chuckled and Luke took the opportunity to bend close and murmur in her ear, "Now you look like you've just rolled out of bed, wild thing."

All she could do was struggle for control and fume silently that he'd managed, once again, to get them photographed while he was scrambling her brains and vaporizing her bones.

But when she stole a sideways glance at him she remembered that he hadn't been as unaffected as he'd appeared. He'd been big and...

hard. Well…everywhere. And for a second he'd
looked at her as though he wanted to take one
big greedy bite out of her before swallowing
her whole.

Whatever his motives, Lilah thought as a fresh
wave of embarrassment heated her cheeks, all
she had to do to get through the rest of the evening with as much dignity as possible was stay
as far away from Dr. Luke Sullivan as she could.

Oh, yes, and hope some other calamity occurred in Spruce Ridge that would draw everyone's attention away from the public spectacle
that was her life.

In the week following that embarrassing dinner,
heat-wave conditions gripped the entire Pacific
North West. Temperatures soared to over a hundred and all ER medics who hadn't succumbed
to the stomach virus were put on some crazy
rotation hours that made med school and residency seem like a Sunday school picnic.

Lilah couldn't help feeling responsible since
she'd prayed for calamity, but she hadn't meant
it to be so…well, potentially disastrous, especially when she suddenly found herself working
at close quarters with the two men she wanted
above all else to avoid. She'd been doing a cred-
ible imitation of ignoring Luke but he seemed to
take perverse pleasure in cornering her during
lulls and scrambling her brains.

When she asked him to stop, he blinked and told her innocently that he was just letting Webster know that she was taken—just like they'd agreed. *Yeah, right*, like he had an innocent bone in his body, Lilah thought darkly. She was not fooled by his sleepy looks, wicked smiles and wickeder kisses—even when they made her forget her own name or why she was supposed to be ignoring him. Besides, she didn't remember any such agreement.

But one thing she did learn about him was that he was an excellent trauma surgeon. He was as steady as a rock and seemed to know instinctively what would work. Lilah guessed it had something to do with years in military ops.

When the heat wave approached the ten-day mark, a state-wide forest-fire warning was announced and County Gen's burn unit was placed on daily alert. Huge areas to the north and south had already been devastated by fires and emergency personnel everywhere were spread pretty thin. Unfortunately, it also meant that in addition to her ER rotation she'd been put on the medevac flight list, even though she'd told the administrator that she got airsick because of inner-ear problems.

She didn't get airsick and her inner ears were fine; she panicked in anything smaller than a commercial jet. Okay, things got freaky then too, but at least they served alcohol on commercial jets. Unfortunately, hospital policy tended to frown on medics hitting the bottle mid-flight.

Then Peter called an emergency meeting to inform them that all medics were required to put in flight hours or face dismissal—which certainly put things into perspective for Lilah. Besides, having someone witness her complete meltdown was preferable to being fired.

But then her rotation finally came and Lilah wondered if being fired wasn't a better option. Especially when she dashed across the roof to the chopper sitting like a giant bug on the helipad, only to find her pilot hunched over, one large hand propped against the metal and breathing like he'd run up sixteen flights of stairs—carrying the chopper.

She gulped as concern—fine, and panic—tightened her chest. "Are you all right?"

He spun round with a snarl, as though he'd been caught doing something illegal and Lilah gasped and stumbled back a couple of steps when she saw who it was—looking like one wrong move from her would trigger a blitz attack.

"L-Luke?" Her voice emerged as a strangled croak. She started forward, pulse skittering with alarm as she took in his ashen pallor, the sheen of moisture covering his face and the wild look in his eyes. "What's wrong? Are you all right?"

"Of course I'm all right," he growled hoarsely.

"Why wouldn't I be?" Muttering irritably, he stuck his head into the engine cavity. He fiddled around, huffing, grunting with an occasional curse before finally emerging, sucking the knuckles of one hand. He was all simmering testosterone and impatient masculinity.

Lilah inhaled shakily as he reached up with his free hand to grasp the engine cover before noticing that she was still standing there, gaping at him. He paused and scowled like he'd expected her to have disappeared.

"What are you doing here?"

She gulped and promptly felt herself go pale. *Darn*. She'd forgotten she was supposed to be getting into the metal bug. She licked dry lips and indicated the emergency meds case at her side. "Flight emergency? I'm on call."

"Oh, right," he said with a frown, as though he'd just remembered. And didn't look too happy about it. Yeah, well, that made two of them.

He turned away, but she swore she heard him grinding his teeth as he yanked open the door and pulled himself into the seat. Completely bemused, Lilah watched as he strapped himself into the harness and fiddled with the control panel—as though he had every intention of piloting the chopper.

She went cold and then hot, and her stomach cramped like she'd caught the stomach flu going around.

"Where's the…um…the pilot?" she gulped, wondering why he was behaving so…well, weird came to mind.

"You're looking at him."

*What?* She felt her head go light and had to steady herself against the chopper's metal frame. "Y-you?" *No way.* She might want to plaster herself up against him but that didn't mean she was going to trust him with her life.

"What?" he demanded, looking like she'd insulted his man code or something. "You have a problem with that?"

"You can…um, fly? A helicopter?"

He growled low in his throat. "Of course I can fly a helicopter. Why the hell do you think I'm in the damn pilot's seat?" And when she continued to gape at him, he growled impatiently, "Get in, we're burning daylight."

"Where's the, um…other pilot? The *real* one?"

"I *am* a real pilot, woman." He heaved an aggravated sigh. "But if you're referring to Granger, he's puking his guts out somewhere. Damn stomach virus," he ended on a muttered curse, and continued to mutter as Lilah shifted her feet and adjusted the meds case shoulder strap. "You want a pilot? I'm it."

"Actually, I… Is this even legal?" she began, but he was too busy flipping switches to pay attention. The engine started with a whine, and when she made no move to get in—she might even have backed off a little—he actually growled at her.

"In or out, Dr. Meredith?"

*Dr. Meredith?* Sucking in a shaky breath and with a silent prayer to the guardian angel of people suffering from flight terror, Lilah scrambled through the open door and strapped herself into the copilot's seat.

She really, *really* hoped he knew what he was doing because she would throw herself from the helicopter rather than have to fly this thing herself. She opened her mouth to point out that she didn't know a thing about helicopters but he was back to scowling menacingly at the controls. Out of the corner of her eye she noticed a muscle flexing in his jaw and hoped that didn't mean he was clueless about what they were for.

Tension rolled off him in waves thick enough to choke on and she once again got the impression that he was holding himself together by sheer iron will. Her belly churned a warning.

"Luke? Are you sure you're okay?"

He gave a huge sigh and turned to scowl at her. "Why do you keep asking that?"

"Well," she said sweetly, refusing to be insulted by the sheer masculine annoyance in his tone. "Maybe because you're grinding your teeth into powder and you're sweating like a pig."

He snarled. "Maybe I'm sweating because this

model of helicopter doesn't come with air-con," he explained through gritted teeth. "Maybe I'm sweating because it's a damn furnace in here. And in case you didn't notice, you're sweating too."

She gulped as her pulse rate bumped up a couple of notches. *That was from sheer terror.*

"Your hands are shaking," she continued, as though he hadn't interrupted. "You're also hyperventilating and your pupils are dilated. If I didn't know better I'd think you were high on something. Or having a panic attack." *Holy cow, she hadn't thought of that.* "Because if you are, then we have a problem." *Forget problem, it was a catastrophe.*

He snorted his opinion of her diagnosis and flexed his fingers, as though restraining himself from throttling her—or maybe to hide the fine tremor in his hands. Snatching his aviator shades out of his pocket he shoved them on his face, clearly done talking. He put on his headset with suppressed violence and turned his attention to the console, completely ignoring her.

After a few moments he pointed to the second headset and yelled, "Put that on," over the rising noise of the engine. "Or you'll be deaf by the time we head back."

With shaking hands, Lilah snatched up the headset and moistened her dry lips. The rotors sped up along with her pulse until she felt a little light-headed. The instant she adjusted the earpieces she heard him say a bunch of confusing things to the control tower. She didn't much care because the chopper lifted with a sickening lurch and she was too busy gagging on terror. Squeezing her eyes shut, Lilah gripped the armrests—and swallowed a whimper.

She heard heavy, labored breathing and thought maybe she was already losing it. But when she cracked open one eye, a quick sideways glance told her Luke looked as bad as she felt. He was sheet-white, his lips were compressed into a tight line and he was gripping the flight stick with white-knuckled hands as though he was afraid it would bite him.

He was also breathing like he was giving birth to a hippo.

"Luke?" She panicked as they cleared the edge of the building, climbing as they went. She inadvertently looked down and her stomach lurched sickeningly. "What's wrong? Is there something wrong with the engine? The steering joystick thingy?"

"Will you just relax?" he snapped, then shrugged his shoulders as though to shake off something heavy and clingy. Like tension? *Or fear?* "Enjoy the damn scenery or something. There's nothing wrong with the engine or the damn cyclic pitch lever."

"Then why are you cursing, and gripping it like it's about to fly off into space?"

"We're nowhere near space and the CPL's bolted to the floor," he said, tight-lipped, and closed his left hand over some other thingy beside the armrest. The instant he touched it the chopper rose sharply and Lilah sucked in an alarmed breath, her grip tightening until her fingers went numb.

"You know what I mean," she squeaked. "What's wrong? And you'd better tell me because I'm freaking out here. And in case you wondered, I'm terrified of flying commercial. This is…this is really scary. In fact, I'm about to completely lose it."

He really looked at her then, and what he saw must have registered because his features relaxed…marginally. "Hey, chill out. I flew choppers in the army for twelve years. I can do this in my sleep." *She really,* really *hoped he wouldn't have to do that.*

"Then why are you so tense?"

"I'm not tense!" he yelled, then sucked in a sharp breath as though he was struggling to get his temper—or maybe his emotions—under control. "I'm just… It's been a while since I've flown."

He fell silent, clearly expecting her to do the same. But Lilah needed a distraction. She watched him inhale through his nose and exhale out his mouth like he was trying to steady his breathing in much the same way she did when she was trying to get a grip. *Great.* She swallowed a terrified sob. *Just great!* Her damn pilot was more nervous than she was.

After regaining control of her vocal cords, she asked as casually as she could, "So…how long? Since you flew, I mean."

His jaw hardened again and after a couple of beats he replied, "Nine months." Reluctantly. As if the admission had been dragged from him by force.

"Nine months?" Nine months didn't seem that long but, then, what did she know? "What happened nine months ago? And remember the first rule when dealing with a potentially hysterical woman," she warned with false lightness. "You lie and say everything's going to be okay."

His mouth relaxed its rigid lines and he chuckled, but it sounded a little scratchy, as though he was trying to laugh through panic. He must have thought so too because a dull flush rose up his neck. He cleared his throat and checked the instruments, adjusting the chopper's course until they were flying northeast.

Away from the city, Lilah noted with a strangled gasp. Away from civilization, and straight for the mountains. Where huge storm clouds hulked like waiting vultures.

"Well?" she prompted, when he'd been silent

for so long that she'd begun to think he didn't intend replying. He sent her a look she couldn't interpret as he was wearing shades, but his taut jaw and uncompromising mouth made Lilah shiver. She could easily imagine him dressed in army fatigues with that badass soldier attitude, flying over hostile territory and dodging ground-to-air missiles.

"I was just wondering what to tell you, that's all."

She didn't think that was all. The big dangerous army guy was as tense as piano wire and probably embarrassed that she would think he was a wimp. *Yeah, right*. Like that was even possible. Not when his blood was probably ninety-nine percent testosterone.

"How about the truth?"

"That's classified."

"Well, how about the PG version, then?" she suggested with a sigh, wondering if all military people were this forthcoming with information. "The version that won't get me killed if I ever get arrested or interrogated by enemy forces."

This time his chuckle was more natural and Lilah felt a flood of relief that left her a little dizzy. Or maybe that was because she'd been holding her breath. She exhaled noisily, feeling absurdly pleased that she'd managed to distract him—and make him smile. Because once he'd relaxed a little she realized he really did look competent handling the controls. Like he knew exactly what he was doing. Which was very good—even if it didn't stop her from freaking out.

"Answer me one question first," he said with a lopsided grin that messed with her breathing and made her pulse rate speed up.

"Sure. What do you want to know?"

"Tiger, leopard or zebra?"

"What?" The abrupt subject change confused her and she turned from her study of the clouds to frown at him. He was grinning at her now, confusing her even more. "What are you talking about?"

"Never mind." He chuckled and turned away. "I can always find out for myself."

Reality dawned and Lilah's eyes widened. While she'd been worried about him—okay, and herself—he'd been imagining her in her underwear?

"Are you talking about my underwear?" she demanded, heat staining her cheekbones when her breasts tightened and her belly gave an interested quiver. "Because we are not discussing that. I'm more interested in why you looked like you were having a stroke when I arrived."

"You're exaggerating." He snorted his opinion of her diagnosis. "I'm just a little dehydrated, that's all," he growled, but his neck darkened as he pretended interest in the controls. "The government doesn't let just anyone fly their aircraft, you know. I'm an excellent pilot with thousands of flight hours." He paused briefly as though choosing his words carefully. "But sometimes equipment failure isn't the only reason choppers crash."

Lilah narrowed her eyes on his carefully blank expression and waited for him to explain. When he didn't, she gasped with dawning horror, "You crashed?" Her belly clenched. "You *crashed*?" She swallowed convulsively when her voice rose a little hysterically. "And now you're scared you're going to crash again." *Oh, God.* This was worse than she'd thought. "*I thought you said you could fly this thing in your sleep*?" she yelled at him, doing a little breathing technique of her own.

"I'm not scared! Jeez," he gritted out irritably.

Lilah could see she'd insulted his manhood again, but she was more interested in the details, so she demanded, "So, why did you crash? Are you all right? Did you suffer any injuries?"

Luke studied her pale face and huge grey eyes. He thought about the long weeks in hospital followed by rehab while waiting for his ribs, leg and hip to heal. Long months during which he relived the crash over and over again, wondering if he could have done things differently. He didn't know and it drove him crazy thinking about it.

"RPGs and I'm fine. But the others…" He paused, thinking about the men who hadn't been so lucky. Good men who'd died protecting the hostage they'd been sent in to retrieve. "Not so much," he said quietly. It haunted him and he felt responsible even though he couldn't have avoided that RPG. But he didn't want to feel responsible for any more deaths. Especially—he looked sideways at the woman staring at him with wide silvery eyes—especially not hers.

There was something about Lilah Meredith that got to him, right in the middle of his chest where it burrowed deep and tightened until he could scarcely breathe. It could just be indigestion, but he suspected it was more. More than her flawless skin and smart mouth. More than her lush curves and the wild rose-colored curls she tried so hard to tame. He suspected it was more than the passion straining to break free of that tight prickly control.

Luke looked into eyes the color of hell smoke and thought that sometimes, when she was unaware of being observed, he caught sight of something soft and fragile and damaged. Something she'd no doubt hotly deny—prickly woman that she was. Something she tried hard to hide behind a smart mouth and a stubborn chin.

Someone had probably done a number on her, Luke decided, fighting the oddest urge find out who it was and hunt them down.

"Hey," he said softly, resisting the urge to touch her—or promise to slay dragons for her. He wasn't a hero, and making promises he couldn't keep was just idiotic. "I'll get you home safely, I promise." Okay, he was officially an idiot. "I'm an excellent pilot." *Finally*. Something he didn't have to lie about.

Lilah's solemn look sent cold shivers up his spine. "What?"

"Some promises," she reminded him quietly, "just can't be kept."

# CHAPTER SIX

LILAH LEFT THE tourist center and eyed the late afternoon sky. While she'd been busy saving lives, angry grey clouds had rolled in, covering the sky and most of the surrounding mountains. It was barely six but the turbulent greenish-black cloud cover made it appear much later.

Fortunately the guy they'd been sent to airlift to County Gen had suffered nothing more than an allergic reaction to something he'd come into contact with when he'd left the trail to relieve himself. It hadn't exactly been the life-saving moment she'd expected but he'd responded rapidly to an adrenalin shot, which was probably a good thing considering his opinion of flying outstripped even hers. It also looked like the heat wave was about to end. Spectacularly too, if those clouds were any indication.

A lump of dread settled in her belly at the thought of getting back on the chopper. Her knees had only just stopped wobbling and she'd finally managed to get her pulse and breathing back to normal.

She rounded the building and spotted Luke almost at once. He wasn't alone and both men had their backs to her as they leaned through the open chopper door. One set of wide shoulders drew her gaze as though magnetized and a small shiver edged up her spine.

She would recognize that broad back and those long legs and narrow hips anywhere. It was probably the way he held himself—that irritatingly appealing mix of masculine arrogance and natural athletic grace. As though he knew who he was and didn't care what the rest of the world thought.

She envied him that, she decided as her gaze traced the long length of his tapering back. That supreme confidence in his ability to handle whatever came his way.

In fact, she could almost hate him for it, she thought with a sigh of feminine envy. *And* for the incredibly tight glutes, showcased to perfection in soft worn denim.

Abruptly aware that she was ogling a man's behind and grinning like a crazy person while thinking hot impure thoughts, Lilah tore her eyes from his butt as heat flooded her cheeks.

*Yeesh, woman. Get a grip.*

Mentally rolling her eyes, she stuck out her bottom lip to blow cool air into her hot face.

*Yikes.* She couldn't remember when she'd last had such an intensely…primitive reaction to anyone. Almost as if he was an industrial magnet that had been turned on high and she a hapless paperclip—drawn to him, in spite of the fact that he was the kind of guy someone like her should avoid like a tax audit.

She couldn't actually remember ever feeling anything like it, and it spooked her. So she sucked in a shaky breath and tried to remind herself that she had no intention of getting all worked up over some hotshot ex-soldier—no matter how sexy. She was an adult, for heaven's sake, not an emotionally fragile adolescent easily impressed by a pair of wide shoulders, long legs and pretty green eyes. She sighed. Not to mention big, long-fingered hands…or awesome pecs and abs…or…or those hot, consuming kisses.

*Oh, boy.*

Embarrassed by her undisciplined thoughts, Lilah willed away the images in her head and the hot flash they gave her. Besides, she really couldn't afford a distraction right now, especially by some rich soldier boy slumming it at a state hospital—no matter how attractive. And, boy, Luke Sullivan was a very attractive distraction; especially bent over a topographical map and frowning while the ranger talked and pointed to something on the map.

*Frowning?*

*Uh-oh.* "Is there a problem?" she asked, half dreading the answer. She really didn't want there to be a problem.

Both men turned and Luke opened his mouth to reply but his gaze narrowed as he zeroed in on her face. He straightened abruptly and rapidly scanned the surroundings. "What's wrong?" he demanded. "Is everything okay?"

Lilah gaped at him, momentarily taken aback by the swift change from relaxed to coiled alertness. Like a large predator sensing danger. Or maybe a seasoned soldier anticipating a sneak attack.

"Uh…fine?" she squeaked, looking over her shoulder. Her pulse skittered with alarm and she half expected to see a grizzly lumbering after her. When she saw nothing but a half-empty lot surrounded by forest, she edged closer to the two men, just in case.

"How's the patient?"

"Who?"

His mouth curved and an eyebrow rose up his forehead. "The guy you flew here to save," he reminded her.

"Oh, Mr. Kemp's fine," she murmured absently, turning from her nervous survey of the surroundings to find two large alpha males regarding her with varying degrees of amusement. *What? Oh, right, they were talking about the allergy guy.* "He…um…he just ignored the rule about staying out of thickly wooded areas and developed an allergic reaction." That was the understatement of the year. The guy had swelled up to the size of a blimp and he'd had huge welts all over his body. "Anyway, he responded to the adrenalin shot. He'll make a full recovery."

"You signed him off?"

"I kept an eye on him for a few hours," she explained. "Most of the swelling has gone down. Besides, he refused a trip to hospital." Not that she could blame him. "His wife took him back to their camp site to sleep off the antihistamine I gave him. But don't worry, I got them both to sign the waiver before they completed the paperwork."

Luke studied her silently for a couple of beats. "Then why are you flushed? Are you sick?"

"What?" She patted her cheeks and tried not to look guilty but his gaze sharpened on her as though something had occurred to him.

"Did something happen? Those hikers in the info center were pretty mouthy. Did they give you a hard time?"

Lilah stared at him in fascination. She could easily imagine him going into the restaurant and kicking some serious butt if she said yes. "I think they left." When he continued to study her silently, Lilah's flush deepened and she felt as though he knew she'd been ogling his backside. She licked her lips and her gaze flicked nervously to the ranger watching their exchange with interest. *Oh, God, please don't tell me I'm that transparent. How embarrassing.*

"Hi," he said, "I'm Jeff."

She replied with "Um…hello," as if she was thirteen and had forgotten how to use her voice. She mentally rolled her eyes and prayed something happened so they would stop watching her like they expected her to do something interesting. She shifted restlessly beneath speculative appraisal and wished for divine intervention. Or maybe that grizzly.

"I'm parched," she lied breathlessly, when it was clear they were waiting for her to say something, but her stomach decided to growl loudly at that moment. She pressed a hand to it, hoping they hadn't heard, but when Luke's eyes gleamed with amusement she knew her prayers were just not getting through.

"More like starved," he observed dryly. "Sounds like you need to be fed."

Since that made her sound like a pet, Lilah decided to shift everyone's attention away from her red face and growling stomach. She gestured to the map. "So…what's with the map? Are we flying anywhere else?" *Please, say no.*

After one last probing look Luke reached into a cooler and emerged with a cool drink. He shook his head and relieved her of the steel case, only to replace it with a cold can.

"Too dangerous," he said absently. "The storm's going to hit soon and Jeff just got off the radio with Spruce Ridge. There's a lot of lightning and even if we leave now, we'd be flying straight into it."

"Oh," Lilah said, frowning down at the cold, sweating can in her hand as though she'd never seen one before, when what she was thinking was, *Thank goodness*! She glanced up. "We can't fly around it or something?"

Luke snorted and snatched the can from her hand, flipping the tab before he handed it back. "Look around you, babe," he said with barely concealed impatience. "Which way would you suggest we go?"

*Babe?* She looked around and wondered if she'd missed something. Like a couple of chalets hidden away somewhere. "But—"

"You really want to fly in that?" Luke demanded, and when Lilah paled and sent him a horrified look he snorted and drawled, "Didn't think so. So what's the problem? Big fancy date?"

She had a feeling he was talking about Peter, and barely resisted the urge to throw the opened can at him.

"Nothing that can't be rescheduled," she lied smoothly, turning away to lift the drink to her mouth, hopefully covering any tell-tale signs of prevarication. The man had eyes like a hawk.

She wouldn't be surprised if he had x-ray vision and could see every lie before it formed. *Yikes*. What a notion.

Besides, what woman wanted a hot guy to know that she didn't have a date on a Friday night? That's right. *None*. Not unless she wanted to look like a dateless loser. Which—come to think of it—described her life perfectly.

"Good," he said shortly, turning away to begin folding the map with barely concealed irritation, and Lilah had to physically restrain herself from sticking out her tongue at him. "Jeff says there's a nearby ranger cabin we can use. The present owner is away and won't mind us spending the night."

"Oh," she said, surprised by the offer. "Thank you." *Us?* "That's great." *God help me*. To cover her reaction she lifted the can to her mouth and chugged back a third of the drink.

"It's pretty rustic," Jeff warned, "but at least it's got a bed and a hot shower."

A bed? As in one? Lilah gulped and flicked a glance at Luke, catching him watching her with an unreadable expression. Her heart gave one slow tumble in her chest before setting off like a bat out of hell. *If there's one bed...where is he...?* A smile tugged at one corner of his mouth, as though he knew exactly what she was thinking. And was hugely amused. *The rat*.

Lilah felt her cheeks catch fire and her breath

stall in her throat as his gaze turned hot. *H-o-l-y cow!* Her pulse rate rocketed into orbit but she narrowed her eyes in a that's-what-you-think-pal look before turning to Jeff with a smile that was much warmer and brighter than she'd intended. "I'm sure it's wonderful. It has to be better than sleeping in the chopper."

Three hours later, Luke sank onto the bed and wondered if he was losing his mind. He'd turned down going out with the guys for this. This being having the object of his hotter-than-scorching fantasies just across the very narrow hallway. In a very small cabin. All night. Probably naked.

Sighing, he lifted one booted foot to rest on his opposite knee and reached for the laces. Halfway through dinner he'd seriously considered going back to the chopper. Even with the storm battering the area like a prelude to Noah's flood, it had to be safer—and certainly smarter—than spending the night with a woman he couldn't get out of his head. A woman who smiled and flirted with forest rangers like she'd never smiled and flirted with him. A woman who drove him nuts even when she was dressed in wrinkled scrubs.

He scowled and pulled off his boot. It dropped onto the floor with a thud. Maybe that was the problem, he mused. Now that he knew what she hid beneath those shapeless scrubs, all he could think about was getting her out of them.

*But she clearly preferred guys in uniform,* he told himself. *Which meant she was looking for a hero—just like every other woman.*

And, God knew, he was no hero.

Scrubbing his hands over his face, Luke's jaw tightened when he recalled her catching him hunched over and panicking like a girl. He pulled off his other boot with a snort of disgust. One look at the chopper and he'd gone all woozy, which had been damn embarrassing. The only thing that had saved his ass from a full-blown flashback episode had been the realization that she was more terrified than he was.

Dropping his boot to the floor, he rose to strip off his shirt just as lightning flashed and the air outside exploded. The ground trembled beneath the assault, rain battering the small cabin as though determined to wash everything away.

The next instant an ear-splitting scream abruptly sent the hair on the back of his neck shooting straight up. By the time he'd thought, *Lilah!* he'd vaulted over the bed, yanked open the door and leapt across the hallway.

He slammed open her door and crouched in the doorway, tensing in anticipation of an attack. Expecting to see her in the clutches of terrorists or at least a family of crazed raccoons, Luke was surprised to find her balanced on top of the bed, clutching a pillow and looking like she'd just seen Jack the Ripper in action.

"What? Where—?" he demanded, momentarily distracted by the sight of her in nothing but a pair of very brief lilac panties and a tight white tank. His eyes widened. *Whoa!*

Her head swung in his direction and with a squeak she launched herself at him, wrapping her arms and legs around him as though she wanted to climb up his body like a capuchin monkey.

Instinctively closing his arms around her, Luke staggered backwards under the full force of her surprise attack. When he collided with the passage wall, he found his arms full of silky, warm woman—his face an inch away from a soft, fragrant cleavage.

*Whoa*, he thought again as blood rushed to his head and he experienced momentary dizziness. *Fine*, he was light-headed from it rushing south without his permission. He was a red-blooded male, *dammit*. Who hadn't had sex in—well, never mind how long! Besides, it could just as easily be because she had a death grip around his neck.

"*Killitkillitkillit*," she squeaked in terror, tightening her grip with every syllable.

"Wha—?" he croaked, his eyes almost crossing when she wriggled against him and sent his blood pressure shooting through the top of his head.

He tried to loosen her death grip so he could breathe—or get the blood back to his brain before she noticed he was getting aroused.

"Oh, my God!" Lilah squeaked, trembling. "It's a…it's a… It's *huge*."

Luke's eyes widened and his mouth curved in a smirk of pride. Well, of course it was huge but he didn't like to brag. In fact, he—

"Kill it!" She interrupted his smug musing.

*Kill it?*

Lilah hid her face against his neck and shuddered, though not in a good way. It should have been his first clue that she wasn't a woman beside herself with lust. In fact, she was whimpering.

*What the—?*

Deciding he needed to see her expression before his ego suffered irreparable damage Luke grasped her shoulders and eased her back a little.

"What are you babbling about?"

Lilah pressed closer. "S-s-s—" She shuddered, and gulped. "S-snake."

"Snake?" Luke demanded hoarsely, as relief washed away the alarm. He gave a strangled laugh. *Jeez, for one second there he'd thought—* "Why the hell didn't you say so in the first place? I thought you were being attacked by tangos."

"Wha-at?"

"Terrorists," he explained, sliding his hands up her smooth thighs to her bottom, which he squeezed before easing her away. *What the heck are you doing?* an inner voice demanded. *Don't tell me you're going to get all honorable, especially with that firm, silky bounty filling your hands?* But there he was, preparing to be noble. *What an idiot.* He sighed. "So where's this huge snake?"

Lilah pointed behind her towards her room and swallowed. "C-corner, near the window."

"Did it bite you?"

Lilah gave a shudder and for one awful moment Luke thought it had, then she shook her head and he exhaled in a silent whoosh. Pulling free of her stranglehold, he set her down and immediately felt the loss of all that soft feminine warmth. He sighed and wondered if he'd lost his mind. But it was probably for the best. His brain wasn't exactly working well if he could mistake revulsion for…well, never mind what he'd mistaken it for.

He'd clearly lost his mind.

Luke turned away and Lilah wanted to call him back or tell him to be careful, but her vocal cords were frozen. She watched him disappear and reappear almost immediately. His unexpected reappearance made her jump about a foot in the air and utter an embarrassing squeak. Mortified, she slapped a hand over her mouth and blinked at him when he sent her a what-the-heck-is-wrong-with-you-woman? look.

"I'm going to flush it out," he explained, as though to a crazy person, and she noticed for the first time that he was holding out her sneaker. As if he expected her to take it. What the heck was she supposed to do with one sneaker?

"If it escapes out the door, hit it with this."

*What?* Lilah felt her eyes widen. She gaped at him like he was the crazy person. "Are you insane?" she squeaked. "What if…what if it's a spitting cobra or…or worse?"

Luke shook his head and lifted his free hand to grip the top of the doorframe as though he needed to keep his hands busy. It made every well-defined muscle in his torso ripple and tighten.

*Yu…humm!* She licked her lips.

For long silent beats he stared at her like she was giving him a headache, which was kind of rude considering she could barely concentrate on anything other than his unfastened low-riding jeans. *Wow. And all that yummy exposed… hard…satiny smooth…flesh.* She was having a hot flush—or coming down with something terminal—just looking at him.

*Yeah*, a voice snickered in her head. *The terminal hots for Dr. Hot 'n' Sexy.*

*Great.* Now she was hearing voices too.

Something came at her. She gave another startled squeak and slammed her eyes shut. After a long silence she heard him say, *"Lilah!"* sounding extremely exasperated, and cracked open one eye to find him smirking. *The jerk*.

"Won't you need that?" she asked nervously, making no move to take the sneaker he proffered. Taking it meant she accepted the implied responsibility and there was no way... She snatched it from his hand before he was tempted to use it on her.

With a final hooded look in her direction he disappeared into the room. Almost immediately she heard him moving furniture around and then there was a lot of banging and swearing. It was followed by a short silence during which Lilah held her breath and waited, only to have it escape in a noisy whoosh when he appeared in the doorway, scowling and sucking his right hand.

"Damn thing bit me," he said, sounding outraged, and Lilah stumbled back a step, feeling abruptly woozy.

"Wha—?"

He looked down at his hand, where a row of small puncture wounds welled blood. "Dammit. I was only trying to save the little sh... sucker. And it bit me." He glared at the offending wounds as if he couldn't believe it had happened then lifted his gaze to glare at her like it was her fault. "I haven't been bitten since... Are you going to faint?"

Spots appeared in Lilah's vision until she realized she was on the verge of passing out. She sucked in a shaky breath and when oxygen hit her brain she panicked. "Ohmigod, it bit you? Where's the antivenin kit? Are you going to die? Where's your gun? Where's your hunting knife? Did you kill it?"

Luke's gaze widened. "Are you nuts?" he demanded. "You don't just go around shooting and filleting defenseless wildlife. In case you haven't noticed, we're in a national park."

She stared at him in confusion. *So?* "But... but it's a...snake." She shuddered. "And it bit you. I saw it. That thing's eight foot long and venomous."

"What, this little thing?" he snorted, and brought his left hand from behind his back. And he was holding—Lilah shrieked and lurched backwards—a wriggling black and red snake. And before she knew what she was doing she drew back her hand and threw her sneaker at it—nailing Luke square in the groin.

He made an odd whooshing sound in his throat, doubled over and dropped to his knees. The next thing she knew, the snake—suddenly finding itself free—streaked off down the passage and disappeared into the kitchen.

"Ohmigod, *ohmigod*!" she squeaked, using his hunched-over body as a shield. Clutching his shoulders, she heard herself whimpering, "It got away." Then reality dawned and she shrieked, "*You let it get away!*"

It was hugely embarrassing to be losing it in front of him so she bit her lip then bit his shoulder since it was his fault the darned thing had escaped. Then it dawned on her that it was slithering free in the house. She punched him. "*Why the hell did you let it get away?*"

Luke made a choking sound and his body shook, abruptly reminding Lilah that he'd been bitten. By a snake. She shuddered. *He'd been bitten.* And was going into shock.

Suddenly remembering that she was a doctor and that she'd treated a host of snake bites during her months in South America, Lilah morphed into ER mode.

First she had to make him comfortable. "Luke?" And then…*oh, God*…she'd have to deal with the convulsions. "Luke?" she demanded a little louder, and tugged him towards her. The snake must be highly toxic if he was already going into cardiac arrest.

"*Luke!*"

She finally got a good look at his face and her eyes widened. She gaped at him for a couple of beats, finally comprehending that while she'd been freaking out that he was going to die he'd been…he'd been… "Laughing?"

She shoved him away from her as though he'd

grown fangs and sprouted scales. "You're laughing?" she demanded, and Luke slumped against the wall to grin up at her.

"How can you laugh at…at…?" she stuttered in rising fury, glaring down at him with her hands on her hips. "You…you…." And since she couldn't think of a bad enough name to call him, she sucked in a steadying breath and pointed a shaking finger at him. "*Jerk*!"

"*Ohmigod*," he gasped in a strangled falsetto. "It bit you. Where's your gun? Where's your big soldier knife? Are you gonna die?"

He snorted and tried to control himself but when Lilah narrowed her eyes he howled with laughter. She finally snatched up her sneaker and threw it at him but this time he plucked it out of the air before it could damage anything important.

He paused, snickering rudely. "You're real cute when you get all flustered at the sight of a little snake, Doc. Didn't you just get back from the jungles of South America? The last time I looked they had huge mothers there."

She ignored his reference to South America. Not going there. "Congratulations," she said sarcastically instead, "you just let a poisonous reptile get away. You…you…*dumb-ass*!"

He looked up from inspecting his bleeding hand to grin at her. "What, like a giant spitting cobra?" Lilah glared at him from a distance, not trusting herself to get any closer. She might accidentally kick him.

He snickered. "Relax. It wasn't poisonous."

"How do you know?"

He looked up at her, his brow arched with amused masculine superiority that was damn annoying. "I'm an army ranger. You get to know stuff like snakes."

"It could still poison you."

Luke held out his hand. "Wanna suck it from my body? Save me from an agonizing death?"

"No," she snapped, sending him the kind of look women had perfected when they thought you were a dumb-ass too stupid to live. "I'm going to find a first-aid kit and you're going to find that snake."

Luke frowned up at her with stunned disbelief. "And do what with it?"

Her departing look told him exactly what he could do with it. All she said was, "Kill it, chop it up into sushi bits and eat it, I don't care. *As long as you get rid of it.*"

Luke watched her lilac bottom sway as she stomped down the passage and disappeared into the bathroom. He winced when the door slammed behind her. He didn't know why she was all bent out of shape. It wasn't like she'd been the one bitten—he snorted—by a little ringneck.

Rising to his feet, he called out, "Tastes just like chicken," over his shoulder, as he headed down the passage towards the kitchen. "It's an excellent form of protein."

# CHAPTER SEVEN

IT TOOK LUKE about twenty minutes to find, corner and then catch the damn snake—without being bitten. But this time he'd been smart about it. He'd found a mop and a bucket in one of the kitchen cupboards and then hunted it down like a mission operation.

And all the way through the banging and swearing, he kept remembering the way Lilah had looked standing on the bed, eyes huge as dinner plates with those tiny bikini panties exposing her long slender legs and flat belly, and snug tank molded to her naked breasts like cling wrap.

He caught himself grinning like a moron and chuckled when he remembered her throwing her sneaker at him. Good thing she had terrible aim or she'd have put him out of action for a while.

Not that he'd seen any action—that kind, anyway—in a good long while. It was no wonder he was dreaming about huge smoky eyes, soft lips and lush…curves.

He sighed. The woman was making him crazy.

Eyeing the snake at the bottom of the bucket with disgust, Luke slammed the lid on it and went to get his boots. This little sucker was going outside, rain or no rain.

By the time he returned he was freezing and water streamed down his bare chest, arms and soaked jeans, adding to the puddle already collecting around his boots.

He wiped rain off his face and noticed that Lilah had emerged from the bathroom. She was perched on a stool at the kitchen counter with an array of medical supplies spread out on a clean towel and a water tumbler filled with red wine at her elbow.

He wondered if their host had anything stronger than wine then decided getting drunk probably wasn't a good idea. Alcohol and unrequited lust didn't mix well.

Sweeping his gaze down the elegant line of her spine, he discovered that she'd dressed—which was a damn shame. He kind of liked seeing her in a tight tank and tiny silk panties. She hadn't looked all prim and uptight, not like when she was being cool and professional.

Damn. Now front and center of his brain was an image of her in nothing but her underwear beneath a lab coat. His blood instantly heated, turning the water on his skin to steam. He could almost hear it sizzle as it evaporated.

Toeing off his boots, he said, "Looks like you're waiting for a medical emergency," and reached for his jeans zipper as she turned. "Did something happen?"

Her mouth dropped open and her gaze zeroed in on his hands. After a stunned moment her eyes widened even more. "What...what are you doing?" she squeaked.

Luke paused in the process of unzipping his jeans and glanced up to see if she was serious. "I'm taking off my pants," he drawled, enjoying the wild color flooding her cheeks as her gaze slowly moved up his chest to his face.

*"Wha-at?"* She blinked, as though coming out of a trance. "But...why? You were bitten on your hand. Oh, God, did it bite y—?"

"My jeans are soaked and I'm dripping all over the floor," he interrupted, and pushed the heavy wet fabric down his thighs. "What are you doing?"

Her fascinated gaze tracked his every move and she swallowed hard before stuttering, "I'm... I'm waiting for you?"

"Me?"

She snagged a large towel and lurched off the stool, looking a little shell-shocked. "Yes, I want to look at you," she announced breathlessly. And then, realizing what she'd just said, turned bright red and buried her face in the towel.

She muttered something that sounded like a

curse or maybe a scream and Luke grinned, padding silently towards her. Leaving wet footprints on the floor, he reached out and tugged the towel away from her red face.

"What was that?" he drawled.

Lilah gave a shocked squeak and jumped about a foot in the air when she realized he was inches away instead of across the room. He whipped away the towel, leaving her empty-handed and defenseless. She took one look at him and slapped a hand over her eyes.

"*Ohmigod*, you're…naked."

"Not hardly," he snorted, rubbing his wet hair. "But that can easily be remedied."

Her eyes popped open and skittered around the room as though she didn't quite know where to look. "*No*! I mean I just need to look at your *hand*." Her gaze finally landed on him and she stood indecisively for a moment before firming her mouth.

Luke could literally see her gathering her resolve around her like shield. In the blink of an eye she was suddenly all professional efficiency. Or trying to be, he thought with amusement. She couldn't hide her dismay or the fact that her eyes kept straying over his chest.

"Are you…um, sure that's the only place you were bitten?"

Liking her off balance, he grinned and waggled his eyebrows. "Why? Wanna play doctor and examine me?"

Wild color rose up her neck into her cheeks and he had to suppress an almost violent urge to check where it began—with his mouth. But he didn't think she would appreciate having her scrubs ripped from her body so he could check to see if she was back to wearing a bra and if her breasts blushed along with the rest of her.

She snorted and said sternly, "I don't have to play at being a doctor, you idiot. I am one," but Luke caught sight of the involuntary curving of her mouth. Damn, he liked her smile. It lit her up from the inside and made her eyes sparkle like sunlight off a stormy sea. And he really wanted that soft, wide mouth moving beneath his again. He could practically taste it.

Groaning silently, he wondered wildly what she would do if he yanked her close and devoured her whole. Instead, he found himself chuckling and saying, "Me too. We can take turns being the patient."

Lilah snorted and Luke could see she was trying really hard not to roll her eyes. "In case you've forgotten," she pointed out huskily, "you are the patient." And her voice slid into his veins like a shot of hundred-proof bourbon. It went straight to his head. *And places way south of the border.* So much for not getting drunk.

Feeling a little light-headed, Luke lifted his

arm and frowned at his swollen hand like it was an alien appendage. "It's fine."

Before he knew what she was doing, she'd grabbed his hand and growled, "Dammit, it's not fine. This. Is. *Not*. Fine."

Her touch sent a streak of fire down his spine and he pulled free before he exploded out of his skin. *Jeez*, it felt like his hair was on fire. He felt like it was the first time a woman had put her soft hands on his body and made him harder than a steel spike. He hadn't had this powerful a reaction to a woman's touch since he was sixteen and fooling around with Mary Anne Sherman. No, scratch that. Not even then.

"It's just a scratch," he growled, dropping the towel to rub at his chest and—*jeez*—hide the state of his lower body.

Lilah snorted and rolled her eyes, oblivious to his physical discomfort. "Right, that's why your hand is swelling and you're leaking from a few punctures."

Luke gave a snort, glad to shift the focus from his erection to his hand. *It wasn't the only thing swelling.* "I sound like an inflatable tube."

"Luke!"

He sighed and slung the towel around his neck. "Fine, but I need to dry off. You wouldn't want me catching a chill, now, would you?" Her silvery gaze tracked fire over his chest and suddenly the possibility of his catching cold diminished by another hundred thousand degrees. At this rate he would be having febrile convulsions and dying an agonizing death in less than five seconds.

"I thought big bad military guys didn't catch things like chills? I thought they were too tough."

"We are tough but, in case you forgot, I'm standing here in wet underwear."

Lilah's gaze zoomed south and she blushed when she saw that he was indeed standing there in his underwear.

Which was clinging wetly to his skin.

Leaving absolutely nothing to the imagination. Including the fact that he was big. *Oh, hell.* And hard.

She jerked her gaze upwards, her blush deepening. "Oh, um, right," she squeaked, her tongue emerging to moisten her lips in a move that he felt in his groin like a bolt of lightning.

*Oh, hell,* he thought again. *I'm in deep trouble.*

Lilah gulped and tried not to let her gaze drop further than the awesome pecs at eye level. She squinted at the dog tags around his neck to ground herself when her blood heated to evaporation point and the gas bubbles in her veins made her light-headed.

She swayed closer.

Uttering a tiny mewl of distress, she jerked back. *Damn.* The man was a marvel of physical perfection. He didn't have an ounce of flab anywhere and he was even more impressively ripped up close. The last time she'd seen him this...unclothed she'd been a little preoccupied. The last time they'd been surrounded by curious onlookers and she would have hated someone catching her on camera ogling him like he was dessert. The eye-lock had been bad enough.

And though she'd secretly pored over all those newspapers, the images had been grainy. Even the videos online couldn't do him justice. All they did was hint at his awesomeness.

Besides, she thought, inhaling on a shuddery breath, how could any image capture the damp silkiness of tanned skin or the heat and testosterone that pumped off him like a nuclear reactor? She gulped. She wanted to reach out and touch. She wanted to slide her palms over the hard contours of his body and feel all that...hardness beneath the tight, satiny skin. She wanted to bury her nose in the soft-looking chest hair spanning the area between his coppery masculine nipples and trace the happy trail all the way to—*gulp*—the damp waistband of his black boxer briefs. Boxer briefs that clung to every inch of his impressive erection.

*Oh, boy.*

And all she could think of was their last kiss and the way his mouth had felt sucking at her flesh. And how much she wanted him to do it again. *This time all over.*

"Lilah." His voice was a ragged, low rumble in his chest. It had the same effect as if he'd run his rough tongue up her throat to the tender hollow beneath her ear. Prickly heat broke out all over her body and for some reason she was having trouble breathing. The air around her vibrated, heated, and pressed in on her like a living thing.

*What the heck was happening here?*

*"Lilah."*

"Hmm?" she murmured, preoccupied with the sheer willpower it took not to lean forward and swipe her tongue across one hard, pebbly male nipple. She wanted to taste him. It wouldn't take much effort at all. Just stick out her tongue and… She caught herself licking her lips and swallowed a desperate little moan. *Dammit, woman. Get a grip and stop staring at the man like he's a melting ice-cream cone.*

"Stop looking at me like that," he growled softly, echoing her thoughts. Something in his voice had her finally lifting her gaze up his strong tanned throat to his clenched jaw and firm mouth and finally into his eyes. They were glowing hot and green in the dim light.

Lilah gulped at the need burning up the green. It practically vaporized her on the spot and she went abruptly light-headed—like she'd swallowed too much helium.

"Like what?" she whispered in a husky voice she didn't recognize as her own.

Luke swallowed and Lilah saw his Adam's apple bob convulsively. "Like you want to lick me up one side and down the other," he ground out.

*Oh, can I? Please?* Her heart beat a wild *boom, boom, boom* in her ears and she didn't know what made her do it but she opened her mouth. "You mean like this?" she said in a soft purr as she closed the distance between them and…licked his skin.

*Yu-hum.*

Luke sucked in a sharp breath and closed his hands over her shoulders. Whether to pull her closer or push her away, she didn't know. And when he did neither, she hid a grin of triumph and whispered, "Or maybe like this?" She sank her teeth into his hard, tight pec before opening her mouth and sucking on his flesh. It was hot and smooth—and tasted of rain and…virile man.

His big body shuddered and goose bumps broke out across his chest. Before Lilah quite knew how it happened she was in his arms, and his mouth was all over hers.

Raw need pulsed in the air. It was all around her, against her and inside her too, sending her heart rate rocketing into hyperspeed. It heated her blood as though she'd strayed too close to the sun and was beginning to blaze.

She felt like she'd swallowed a star and any second now her flesh would begin to break apart and the blinding heat and light would leak from the cracks. Then she'd radiate like a supernova and explode all over the place.

His groan vibrated against her skin as he moved towards her mouth, his lips leaving a hot trail across her skin. *Holy hell*, she gasped silently.

The instant before his mouth closed over hers she wondered wildly if she'd wake in the morning with scorch marks on her skin.

Then she ceased to think at all because he had one hand on the back of her head holding her still as his mouth closed over hers, quickly shattering every notion she'd ever had about kissing.

This felt like an invasion—like he'd quit toying with her and was bringing out the big guns. And, boy, was his gun big…and hard…and would have been painful if she wasn't already almost half out of her mind with need.

His slick tongue stroked hers and she finally exploded into action. Groaning low in her throat, she opened her mouth wider and sucked his tongue deeper until he moaned too, low and deep—like he was in pain. His free arm snaked around her back to yank her closer and his kiss became hotter, wilder—more passionate.

And suddenly Lilah couldn't keep her hands to herself. She ate at his mouth and streaked her palms over his shoulders, down his arms and then up his broad back. She loved the feeling of his hard muscles shifting beneath the tight, hot skin and dug her nails into his flesh in an almost primitive desire to mark him.

With a savage growl Luke shifted and before Lilah knew what was happening she was being lifted against him. Instinctively wrapping her legs around his waist, she cried out when the long, thick ridge of him pressed right where she needed it most. Right where she was hot and wet and desperately needy.

Arching her back, she wrenched her mouth free and dragged a ragged breath into her lungs before gasping, "Luke...I don't think we should be...doing...this." His teeth scraped against the delicate skin of her throat and she shuddered. "We really shouldn't." But for some reason she couldn't quite remember why.

"Why not?" he rasped, dragging his mouth along her jaw to nip and suck her ear lobe. He shifted and she became aware that they were moving.

"Because...because—" His lips snatched the word from her mouth, effectively silencing her, and just as effectively snatching every thought from her mind.

"No more talking," he murmured between

kisses, the feel of his words sending fire streaking from her tingling lips to every part of her body, tightening her breasts and pooling between her thighs. "No more thinking. It's hell. And I'm done with hell. I want heaven." He paused and breathed like he was having trouble getting enough oxygen. His gaze was feverish. "And you're going to give it to me."

Lilah moaned. She was having trouble concentrating on anything but the feel of his body against hers. She'd been living her own kind of hell and wanted heaven too. But there was something she should be doing. She was sure of it. Gripping his hair, she pulled his face away and stuttered, "Wha-what about…your hand?" in one last-ditch effort at rationality, because there was another reason why she shouldn't be doing this. But she couldn't remember what it was. Something about frat boys and her father.

He nipped at her mouth, making her squeak and lose her train of thought. "Later," he growled, and for one awful moment she thought he was talking about kissing her. Then the world abruptly tilted and the next instant Lilah found herself flat on her back.

Blinking in confusion, she tried to focus on her surroundings but Luke slid his hands beneath her shirt and all she could concentrate on was how good they felt. She gave a long low groan of pleasure and shifted against him, pressing all her good parts to his even better parts.

His hands were big and warm and calloused, scraping lightly against her sensitized flesh. They made her shiver like she had a chill when she felt anything but chilled. Even so, when he cupped her aching breasts she shuddered and bit her lip against the whimper that rose in her throat.

It escaped anyway as "Oh, God," as she arched helplessly into his big hands.

Luke chuckled deep in his chest. "No, just me. And I'm very human." *Hoo, boy. She could feel just* how *human he was.* Then he was shoving the material up her torso and murmuring, "Look at you, you're so damn beautiful." Her exposed breasts tightened almost painfully and after a long reverent moment he bent and licked one full curve.

Lilah almost came off the bed but his big body pressed her deeper into the mattress as he fed on her flesh, tormenting her with flicking licks and little nips until she wanted to scream—or burst out of her skin. And when he finally sucked one pebbled tip into his hot, wet mouth Lilah cried out and tensed under the onslaught, clutching at his shoulders like he was the only thing keeping her from flying off into space.

Her hands raced over him as he tortured her with his mouth and teeth and when he finally released her nipple it was to drag his open mouth down her belly.

Her skin tingled and quivered. "What are you doing?" she rasped, lifting her head to blink at him and follow his teasing progress.

He smiled against her belly and looked up long enough to drawl chidingly, "Are you sure you're a doctor?"

Breathing heavily, Lilah fell backwards and stared unseeingly at the ceiling. "I think... I think I'm about to become a patient," she gasped, wheezing like a geriatric asthmatic.

Luke chuckled and heaved himself upright until he was straddling her on all fours. He grinned down into her stunned face. "Good thing I know CPR. I'm great at the kiss of life."

She thought, *I know*, but what she said was, "I thought that was chest compressions," and his grin turned wicked as he reached out to run his hand over her chest.

"Oh, yeah." He smirked, fondling the plump curves. "I'm great with that too." Sitting back, he slid his hands down her torso to toy with the waistband of her scrubs before yanking them down her thighs. "And I'm excellent with this." And before Lilah could stop him he'd whipped them past her feet and tossed them somewhere into the darkness.

"Oh, man," he breathed, his hot gaze taking in the sight of her lying there in nothing but a pair of tiny silk panties. Lilah fought the urge to cover herself and tried to remember when she'd last been naked in front of a man. She couldn't and attempted to cover herself but he caught her hands.

"No. I want to see you. You have no idea how often I've wanted to strip you to your underwear." His rough whisper rasped against already exposed nerve endings and she realized he liked what he saw. "See if you were wearing another of your Wild African collection."

"Afric—?" Then she remembered him asking her about tigers and leopards and her breath escaped in a loud *whoosh*. "The helicopter."

His eyes crinkled at the corners. "Yeah, then too. I got hard just thinking about you in leopard-print. But this…?" He paused to toy with the tiny ribbon bow beneath her navel and brush his fingers across her belly until her muscles quivered and heat rushed over her skin. It was like a flash fire settling deep in her belly and creating deep inner ripples of sensation. "This is even better. It makes me want to sit and stare at you all night. And I would," he told her in a rough growl, "if I didn't want to taste what that tiny scrap is hiding."

Lilah swallowed a groan and attempted one last time to think clearly. She was fluttering madly, right where he wanted to…taste? *Yikes*.

"But your hand," she began breathlessly. "It's swollen."

Luke chuckled and pressed his erection against her. Lilah's eyes practically rolled back in her head and her world spun crazily off its axis. She thought she heard him say, "Not nearly as swollen as this," but wasn't certain as there was a tornado roaring through her head.

She bit down on his shoulder, needing somehow to keep herself from being swept up into the vortex, or from whimpering with pleasure as her body went liquid with need.

"Too much," she whispered against the ball of his shoulder. 'It's too much."

His chuckle rumbled deep in his chest, vibrating against her skin where they touched and setting off tiny explosions of sensation. "Not nearly," he murmured wickedly against her hair. "But soon."

Soon couldn't come soon enough for Lilah, especially when he slipped his hands between her thighs and cupped her over the tiny panties. She wanted him, more than she'd ever wanted anyone, and was beyond ready to give him heaven—as long as he took her there too. Then he slid his hand beneath the elastic band to part her slick flesh and Lilah saw stars.

Her breathing hitched and she was afraid she might hyperventilate. Instead, she moaned and pulled him closer, arching into his touch. The need to feel the weight of him against her, and more than his fingers…*there*…was overwhelming. What she wanted was the hot hard length of him inside her, filling her and banishing the aching, hollow loneliness she hadn't even realized she was carrying around.

"I love knowing I can make you lose control when I touch you like this," Luke murmured, nibbling on her ear as he brushed her tiny feminine bump. "Love knowing that I'm soon going to use my tongue on you. Right where I'm touch—"

"Oh, God, stop…*stop* or I'll…" His barely there touch brushed over her again and Lilah sucked in a shocked breath as a powerful orgasm gripped her. She was scarcely aware of his words, murmured against her throat, as his fingers brushed and stroked her through the sensations roaring through her, threatening to blow her head right off her shoulders.

"Oh, God," she rasped, once she could get her lungs working again. "That was… I never felt… You…*huh*." Her breath ran out with a noisy whoosh and she lay there panting and wondering what had hit her.

Luke's face appeared above her and it took her a second to realize they were both naked and his erection was pressing smooth and hot against her thigh.

Luke snatched the hand she hadn't even realized she was moving down his slick abs to her target. "No."

*No?*

"I want to touch you." Lilah pouted. "Besides, it's my turn."

"Later," he growled, sounding like he'd run up the side of a mountain with a hundred pounds on his back. Lilah didn't know whether to growl or cry so she sank her nails into his tight butt. Kind of where she wanted to sink her teeth.

His big body shuddered and he grabbed her hands, lifting them above her head. "Touch me, and it's all over."

Lilah's mouth curved into a slow delighted smile even though her wrists were manacled by one hand while he searched through the bedside table with the other. She decided she liked knowing she could push him to the edge and wondered if he was looking for handcuffs.

She'd never thought being handcuffed would hold such appeal. But that didn't mean she was going to lie there quietly while he got a grip on his control. She wanted him losing it—with her.

"What are you looking for?" she purred, moving against him so their groins rubbed and her nipples brushed his chest. Only the friction made her own breath catch in her throat while tiny clenches deep in her belly started all over again.

*Holy Moses!* That had never happened before.

Once was about all she could usually achieve—
if she was lucky.

"Condom," he gasped, presenting a small foil
packet. Lilah snatched it from him and pushed
him back so she could touch him. Her avid gaze
locked on his impressive erection and she licked
her lips. "Let me," she purred in anticipation, but
he retrieved it just as quickly.

"Not on your life. You touch me and we're
done."

Lilah huffed out a breath and sank back on
her elbows as he ripped open the packet with his
teeth. "I'm on a contraceptive," she whispered
hoarsely, but after a moment's hesitation he
rolled the latex down his thick shaft with shaking hands. Lilah felt her inner muscles clench in
anticipation. *Oh, yes! Come to mamma.*

Finally covered, he looked up and the heat in
his green eyes had her blood surging through
her veins in a way that promptly stole the breath
she'd regained after her first climax.

She licked her lips nervously.

"Now," he said with a slow, wicked grin as
he came down over her and made a place for
himself between her thighs, "let's find heaven
together."

# CHAPTER EIGHT

LILAH CRADLED LUKE'S big hand in hers and gently washed the snake-bite area with warm soapy water. This was something she should have done soon after he'd been bitten and blushed when she recalled why she hadn't.

Frowning at his hand, she probed the red swollen area around the puncture wounds and focused on being a medic. Not an easy task. Not when the heat of his body reminded her of the past couple of hours. Not when every move had her T-shirt—or rather *his* T-shirt—brushing against her tender nipples. Not when she might melt into a little puddle right there on the stool. Or maybe climb onto his lap.

"This looks infected already," she huffed, ducking behind long ropes of tousled curls to escape his too-perceptive gaze. His too-perceptive, *hot* gaze—she corrected with a gulp—currently locked on her face and filled with smoldering heat. She tingled in all the places he'd spent the last couple of hours discovering with his mouth and she didn't have to be a mind reader to know what he was thinking. "Are you sure that snake wasn't poisonous?"

Luke reached out and swept her hair behind her ear as he dipped his head to peer into her face. "Are you blushing?"

"Don't be ridiculous," she said a little breathlessly, dabbing the area dry with an alcohol swab and trying to pretend her face wasn't burning. "It's just a little hot in here."

His chuckle set fire to her nerve endings and further tightened her nipples. Every time she inhaled, she sucked in the potent mix of pheromones and warm male skin. It was wildly intoxicating. And probably why she felt the need to put her mouth on him all over again.

She sneaked a peek and caught him looking at her breasts.

"Do you need a tetanus shot?" she asked breathlessly to distract him and when his gaze moved slowly up her chest, past her chin and lingered briefly on her mouth before finally lifting to hers, she thought she was having a stroke.

His mouth curled at one corner and he shook his head. "Nope. I'm good." *Oh, wow, he certainly was*. Especially when he—*God, no*, she thought wildly, and forced herself to focus on the antibiotic ointment she was applying to the bite area. *Don't think about that.*

Casting around for something to say, she

opened her mouth and, "I'm sorry about…be-fore," popped out before she could stop it.

"Before?"

Lilah licked suddenly dry lips and sneaked another peek. "When I…um…threw my shoe at the snake and…"

"Hit me in the nu—?"

"It was an accident," she interrupted with a spluttered laugh. "I panicked."

Luke smirked. "Good thing you throw like a girl or I'd have been out of action."

"Out of—? Okay, never mind." *Yeesh. Were they really going to discuss that?*

Ducking her head, she hastily covered the wound site with an adhesive bandage before sliding off the stool to prepare a syringe of antibiotics and anti-inflammatory meds. And to move away from the heady scent of his skin. It was making her feel a little drunk. Like she'd been sucking down shooters instead of— He caught her hand and his touch set off deep carnal longing. "I don't need that."

"Yes, you do."

"I already told you—"

"Look," she interrupted testily, and tugged free. "You have no idea where that…that thing had its teeth recently."

"Huh?"

"He lives on the ground, for heaven's sake, and eats dirty little rodents that carry disease.

And no matter what you say," she said, shoving the syringe into the vial of antibiotics, "that thing was poisonous."

"How the hell would you know that?" he demanded with his arms folded across his awesome chest. He was scowling at her like she intended doing something illegal instead of administering a tiny little injection. Lilah snickered. Alpha males were so weird about stuff like needles and injections.

"Please," she scoffed with an eye roll. "The area is swollen and inflamed. Besides, even fifth-graders know that bright colors in nature signal danger."

There was a short silence while she searched for an alcohol swab, then Luke reached out and tugged long strands curling over her breast. "Kind of like you," he drawled with a hot smile that made Lilah's nipples tighten and her insides melt.

"Me?" she squeaked, then laughed because she was the least dangerous person she knew. "I'm not dangerous."

"Oh, yes, you are," he drawled softly, deliberately brushing his knuckles across the tip of her breast as he toyed with a ropey curl. "With hair like this you should come with a warning. *Lethal. Keep far away.*"

She gave a tiny smile. She kind of liked being

thought of as lethal. "Then why didn't you keep far away?"

Luke snorted and said, "I'm an army ranger," as though that should mean something. Rising to his full height, he gently took the syringe and tossed it onto the counter. "We eat danger for breakfast." His smirk reminded her of where he'd had his mouth earlier. "Among other things."

Lilah gulped and got caught in his smoldering gaze. "You do?"

"Uh-huh." He nudged her backwards until she collided with the refrigerator. "And you are very...*very*...dangerous." Planting his palms either side of her head, he leaned down until his mouth was barely an inch away from hers. "But that's okay. I'm trained to handle dangerous... explosions. And now," he growled with a wicked grin, "I'm going to handle you."

She swallowed convulsively and his hot gaze dropped to watch the movement before he finally closed the small gap to kiss her softly and sweetly on her mouth. She gave a tiny moan and parted her lips. The instant her tongue sneaked out to meet his, the kiss exploded and before Lilah knew what was happening, he'd smoothed his big hands up her thighs to her bottom and lifted her off the floor.

The moment Lilah wrapped her legs around his hips Luke freed himself and thrust into her wet heat, groaning when her slick walls clamped down on his shaft. The woman was like a fever in his blood, he thought fiercely, and he couldn't seem to get to the point where he said no more. Maybe he would.

*Later.*

*Much later.*

He briefly considered that it might have something to do with the fact that he hadn't had sex in nearly a year, but he had a very bad feeling that it had nothing to do with sex and everything to do with the woman scraping her nails down his back and sinking her teeth into his shoulder.

Sensation bolted down his spine and about buckled his knees, but Luke tightened his grip on her and thrust again. She cried out, wriggling against him, and his eyes rolled back in his head.

"Don't move," he panted, staggering backwards until his butt hit the counter. Turning with her still crushed tightly against him, he caught her mouth with his, driving his tongue into her mouth.

He'd never before experienced these primitive urges thundering through his veins and making him desperate for the feel of a woman's every tiny quiver and shudder. Primitive urges that made him want to take her hard and fast—and then slow and torturous—and never stop. Lust coiled tight and painful in his groin, as if they hadn't spent the last few hours satisfying both their hungers.

He'd wanted her to show him heaven, and, man…she'd taken him places he'd never gone before. But now that he'd tasted her, felt her around him, he wanted it again. And more. Much more.

Wrenching his mouth from hers, he headed for the sturdy wooden table in the dining area and set her down on the edge. She thrust her fingers into his hair and arched against him, yanking his mouth back to hers. He moaned deep in his throat and smoothed his palms up the long length of her thighs to fill his hands with her soft curves. Yanking her closer, he stilled, marveling at the way they fitted together. Tight and wet and…so damn…*hot*.

The sensations were so intense it was almost enough just to be buried deep. But it wasn't, not when he wanted to move more than he wanted his next breath. Not when she was moaning and moving against him too.

His hungry mouth slanted across hers and he fed her hot ravenous kisses that tightened the knot of tension at the base of his spine. Finally when he could no longer remain still, he broke the kiss and rasped, "*Lilah*" in a voice he didn't recognize as his own. With one sweep of his arm he cleared the table of everything and gently shoved her onto her back.

God, she was beautiful—looking all flushed and rumpled and spread out like his favorite meal.

"Lilah," he rasped again, and grasped the backs of her knees, surging against her until their bodies were locked tight. He did it again. "God," he wheezed, "you make me crazy."

Lilah's husky laugh slid up his spine. "I do?" She smoothed her hand down over her belly to where they were joined and Luke shuddered and surged against her again as though he couldn't get deep enough.

She arched her body and then there were no more thoughts, only heavy breathing and thundering pulses as he pushed her towards release. And when she cried out and clutched at his shoulders as she shuddered and came, he came too, harder than the first or second times. Harder than he'd ever come in his life.

And somewhere in the back of his mind a little alarm bell clanged a warning that he was missing something important. Maybe because he was getting in too deep, that this was too much, too fast. But Luke ignored it. He was too busy fighting for his next breath and basking in the glow of having been to heaven.

The distant sound of banging drew Lilah from a sleep deeper than any she could remember. She briefly considered getting up to see what was going on, but someone had stolen her bones and she couldn't move without immense effort. Sighing dreamily, she snuggled deeper into the bedding and drifted.

The next thing she knew someone was shaking her roughly and murmuring her name in a deep raspy voice. She knew that voice so she hummed and arched languorously beneath the warm touch.

"Lilah," the voice called again, this time a little more firmly, and she frowned irritably. "Wake up. We have an emergency."

Whether from years of conditioning where the word "emergency" had her reacting, or the quiet intensity in that deep voice, Lilah finally found the energy to roll over and open her eyes.

"What's wrong?" she croaked, blinking in the sudden light spilling from the bedside lamp.

She lifted a hand to shove the hair off her face and found Luke leaning over her with one hand planted on the bed and the other molded to her shoulder.

"Get dressed," he ordered, then straightened abruptly as though he hadn't spent the past several hours intimately exploring her body. Despite his detachment, Lilah shivered in memory of that touch. She greedily wanted more. "There's been an accident."

*Accident?* Lilah lurched into a sitting position as he turned away and swept her eyes over him, looking for gaping wounds pumping blood. "How did it happen?" she demanded, her heart pounding just as fast at the thought of him being injured. "Where are you hurt?"

His over-the-shoulder look was hooded even as it scorched a path down her throat and across her naked breasts. "I'm fine," he drawled roughly. "But you'd better get a move on, Dr. Meredith, before I forget about medical emergencies and crawl back into that bed with you." Okay, so maybe he wasn't as distant as he appeared. Which was good. Lilah frowned. Wasn't it?

Belatedly realizing she was as naked as a newborn, she flushed and dived for the covers, but Luke had already gone. Besides, it was a little late to be freaking out about being naked in front of Dr. Big and Buff. The man had already seen every inch of her body and had touched all of her with his hands and his mouth. Several times.

Shoving aside the memories of exactly where he'd had his hands and mouth, Lilah threw back the covers and quickly dressed.

Within a minute she was shoving her feet into her sneakers on her way out the room. She found Luke waiting at the open front door, holding the steel meds case and talking in undertones to a park ranger Lilah hadn't seen before.

"How bad is it?" she asked, twisting her hair into a messy topknot and securing it with her fastener. She peered out into the dark. It was still pouring.

"Don't know the details," Luke said, holding out a rain jacket. "But Danny said Jeff's pretty bad. They're bringing him in now."

Lilah took the slicker from him as he herded her out the door. "Jeff?" she asked, looking over her left shoulder and up into the shadowed face of the man who'd not so long ago swept her off her feet and robbed her of her sanity. "The guy who lent us the cabin? What happened?"

"Long story," Luke said abruptly, and pulled the jacket over her head. "Can you run?"

Without replying, Lilah leapt off the veranda and dashed through the mud to the SUV. The ranger was holding open the rear door and when Lilah dived inside he slammed it shut. Within seconds they were on the move, Danny muscling the vehicle round corners and sliding through puddles. Rain pounded the roof and the wipers swished through the deluge as the vehicle skidded and slid over the muddy terrain.

"Where are we going?" Lilah demanded, grabbing hold of the seats in front of her to keep from being tossed around like a shirt in a tumble drier.

"Ranger station," Luke replied. "It's closer to the chopper and has emergency med supplies."

"I've seen the med supplies," Lilah told Luke. "They won't help if the injury is life-threatening."

"Then we improvise." His profile glowed green from the dash lights as he flashed her an odd look over his shoulder. Lilah felt a warning skate up the length of her spine. It raised the hair at the back of her neck and sent goose bumps rolling over her flesh. Pressing a hand to the ball of tension cramping her stomach, she wondered what they would do if Jeff's injury was critical.

She had an awful feeling she knew.

Within minutes they were sliding to a stop near the rangers' center. Another vehicle was already there and someone waited at the top of the stairs with a flashlight.

"What happened to the power?" Lilah asked as she dashed up the stairs.

"Went out about fifteen minutes ago." *Lovely*, she thought dryly. *Just what we need to make things easy.*

"How is he?" she asked, following him as he turned and headed into the dark building.

"He's lost a lot of blood and is struggling to breathe. I left Frank in there with him."

"What happened?" Luke demanded, appearing out of the darkness behind her.

"We went to check on the bridge over the gorge," the park ranger said. "I heard Jeff shout something as he stepped off the road and the next thing he was gone. By the time we reached him he was struggling with a couple of downed trees. I didn't realize he was trying to pull a broken branch out of his chest until it was too late."

Lilah sucked in a shocked breath. All she could think of was Jeff as he'd been earlier. Alive. Vital. And smiling.

Luke muttered a choice epithet and Lilah knew what he was thinking. The last thing a victim should do was the first they thought of— remove the object from their bodies. Often, what was impaling them was also keeping them from bleeding out.

And then she hurried into a room lit with dozens of candles and lanterns and saw that someone had cleared the table at the front of the room and placed Jeff on it. Her first thought was that it looked like a sacrificial altar and shivered, hoping it wasn't an omen, but even from the doorway she could hear the dreadful wheeze and rattle as he struggled to breathe.

Hurrying towards him, she was aware of one thing. If they didn't plug that hole, the pressure in Jeff's chest would crush his lungs and he'd go into cardiac arrest even before he could bleed out.

Lilah had seen this kind of injury only once and, like before, as Jeff tried to breathe, the air was leaking into his chest cavity and putting pressure on his heart and lungs.

"Check for tension pneumothorax while I examine his wound," Luke said abruptly, automatically taking charge, and Lilah was glad to let him. She whipped her stethoscope around her neck as he removed the makeshift pressure bandage to cut away Jeff's blood-and-rain-soaked khaki shirt.

Aware of Luke's proximity and his calm assurance, Lilah flattened two fingers and palpated the chest, moving every few inches to repeat the procedure.

"Hyper-resonant on the injured side," she announced, checking Jeff's pulse rate one-handed while inserting the stethoscope earpieces into her ears. She slid the disc over his chest and listened. "Unaffected side fairly normal at this stage," she reported, shifting the stethoscope to the side of his injury. "Absent breath sound on affected side." She looked up briefly. "Tachycardia present and integrity compromised."

"*Damn*," he muttered softly, his eyes catching and holding hers. "Three broken ribs," he reported. "Pleura penetration and I'm not sure but it feels like foreign material in the wound."

He turned to the ranger hovering nearby. "Danny, get me a sharp knife, a water bottle and a roll of cling wrap." His gaze returned to Lilah. "Keep an eye on his vitals. Clean the wound as best you can and seal it with plastic wrap."

"Where are you going?"

"The helo." And before she could ask why, he'd grabbed the nearest flashlight and was gone, disappearing into the darkness as silently as a shadow.

By the time Danny reappeared carrying a wicked-looking nine-inch filleting knife, Lilah had cleaned the wound and found a roll of surgical tape. Normally she had all the equipment and supplies of a large hospital at her disposal. Normally she had light and all the proper instruments.

She was now working practically blind with kitchen utensils. Fortunately, Luke's solution would stop air from being sucked in through the wound and a thoracostomy would release the trapped air into the water bottle, creating a vacuum of sorts.

Tearing off a section of plastic, she asked the shaky ranger to hold it in place while she cut strips of surgical tape, which she pressed along the edges. Wanting to give the older ranger something to do, she sent him to the restroom for some paper toweling.

While they waited for Luke's return, Lilah rummaged through the meager supplies and tried to calm an agitated patient whose every breath was a struggle. He tried to talk but she squeezed his shoulder, warning him to save his breath.

He reached out. "I—need—to—tell—"

"You need to stay quiet and still," she said firmly, pressing his arm to the table. "It's going to be okay, Jeff. Just relax and let us take care of things."

"But—"

"Here's the p-paper towel," the ranger stuttered as he returned with the entire roll. Lilah's mouth dropped open.

"What did you do, break open the dispenser?"

"I...I thought it would be more s-sterile if I b-brought the whole thing," he stuttered, rubbing a hand over his hair to the back of his neck in embarrassment.

"Oh. Well...um, good thinking," Lilah said, as a huge hulking shadow materialized beside her. She jolted with fright until she realized it was Luke. *Yikes*, the man was like a ninja. Even six feet four and dripping water all over the floor, he moved like he was materializing from another dimension.

It reminded her that he'd been in elite ops and had likely treated a lot of field injuries, most likely a lot worse than this. But then he was dumping supplies out onto the strips of paper toweling she'd laid out and her mind shut out everything but the task ahead.

"I'm going to make an incision just beneath the armpit," he said, tearing open a box of latex gloves. She took two from him and shoved her hands into them before accepting a packaged

syringe and needle. "Give him a local around
the fifth intercostal."

Lilah quickly stripped off the packaging and
pushed the syringe into the vial of anesthetic,
recalling the syringe filled with antibiotics and
anti-inflammatories she'd administered earlier.
After they'd— As though tuned to her emotions,
Luke turned from giving the older ranger in-
struction on how on to fit and operate the manual resuscitator.

"You okay?" he asked near her ear, as she
swiped a small area with an alcohol swab. She
told herself it was the sound of snapping latex
that made her jolt, but couldn't make herself believe it. He'd spent the better part of the night
exploring her body and now knew her more intimately than her gynecologist. She didn't know
how she felt about that.

"I'm fine," she said coolly. "This should be
ready to go in a couple of minutes. What about
a ketamine shot? He's a little agitated."

"All right," Luke said absently as he unwound
a length of cannula tubing. "Give him thirty
ccs."

"Ketamine?" Danny asked, holding Jeff down
as Lilah prepped another syringe. "Won't morphine be better?"

"No," she said absently, checking for air bubbles. "It's a pulmonary suppressor. Ketamine
will help take the edge off without affecting his

breathing even more until we can get him to a hospital." She gestured for Danny to turn Jeff on his side, soothing the ranger when he let out a ragged groan. She finally turned to Luke. "We're going to fly him out, aren't we?"

His brief look was indecipherable but Lilah's heart gave a painful squeeze. After a short pause he gently lifted the arm on Jeff's injured side. "Danny, help Dr. Meredith hold him while I make the incision."

Lilah followed instructions and watched Luke's long fingers probe the fifth intercostal space in the mid-axillary line. Once he was happy with the position, he placed the tip of the filleting knife where his fingers had been and gave a quick, firm push. Blood instantly welled from the incision, which Lilah readily swabbed.

"Widen the incision site and pierce through the pleura if you can," Luke said, reaching for the cannula tubing.

Lilah murmured soothingly while she maneuvered Jeff until she could press her finger into the incision site. She gently rotated her finger to check for any obstacles and her careful pressure was met with only slight resistance. She pushed harder and waited for Luke to position the cannula before sliding her finger out. Within seconds Luke had inserted six inches of tubing, which he'd already attached and sealed to the plastic bottle. It would now be up to Lilah to close the entry site.

After prepping the suture kit, she set about stitching the area around the cannula to minimize leakage. Carefully drawing the filament thread as tightly as she could without tearing the skin, she tied off the thread and snipped it.

Straightening, she held her breath and eyed the bottle. After a couple of beats foamy bubbles began forming in the water. She quietly exhaled.

"Set up Ringer's lactate in the cubital vein while I dress this," Luke said calmly, nodding to the eighteen-gauge catheter and bag of fluid. "Then we're out of here."

Lilah efficiently set up the drip, her hands quickly performing the task despite the blood draining from her head at the news. "We're really going?" she asked, trying not to freak out at the thought of flying through the mountains in the dark. "What about the storm?"

There was a short tension-filled silence until she looked up and caught Luke staring at her with a hard jaw and steady eyes. "What about it?"

"I…uh," Lilah stuttered, as her heart leapt into her throat. *Oh, help.*

"We can't wait," Luke reminded her quietly, and Lilah felt a little dizzy as she drew in a shaky breath. She swiped her tongue over suddenly dry lips, recalling her embarrassing behavior on the flight in. But embarrassment aside, she could already feel her heart rate increasing and the band of tension around her head tightening.

"Are you going to be okay?" he asked. "I can take Danny if it's a problem." Lilah pressed her lips together and shook her head. There was no way he was leaving her behind. He couldn't fly and tend to a critical patient. That's why pilots flew with medics.

"You're not leaving me behind," she said a little more firmly than she felt, and repacked the supplies as the men transferred Jeff to the stretcher. "Besides, it's my flight call."

"It's bad out there," he warned. "Are you sure you'll be able to handle it?"

Lilah paled as they moved quickly through the building. *Heck, no!* "Can you?"

Luke gave a harsh laugh as they stepped onto the veranda. "Me?" Lilah saw his mouth twist into an ironic smile. "I'm an army ranger, remember."

# CHAPTER NINE

WIND WHIPPED LILAH'S wet hair into her face as she scrambled into the chopper. Moments later the stretcher appeared through the doorway and she reached over to help slide and snap it into place.

While Luke strapped himself into the pilot's seat she attached the bag to an overhead hook and tried to ignore the rising whine of the engine. The rotors began to turn and she looked out the window in time to see the rangers duck out of the way and dash back towards the building. The entire aircraft began vibrating and the sound was deafening, setting her teeth on edge, but she forced herself to focus on wrapping the BP cuff around Jeff's arm and not on the rising pitch of the rotors. If she did she might lose it.

The idea that in a couple of minutes they would be flying through the storm sent a shudder of terror right through her. Her mother had died in a light plane crash on a night like this and Lilah tried not to think that she might as well.

Turning on the battery-operated light, she concentrated on maintaining the rhythm of the manual resuscitator with one hand while activating the electronic cuff with the other. She might have managed to fool her hands into thinking they weren't shaking but she jumped about a foot in the air when someone gripped her shoulder. Realizing she was acting like a crazy person, she looked up a little guiltily.

"You okay?" Luke shouted, his gaze unreadable.

Instead of answering, she nodded and dropped her attention to the headset he was holding out. *No way was she admitting that she was close to freaking out.* "Put it on," he yelled over the rotors. "I need constant updates."

Lilah nodded and slipped the headset over her ears with shaking hands. The roar of the engine immediately lessened and his deep voice filled her head.

"Status," he barked as the chopper rose off the ground with a jolt, and Lilah wondered if he was trying to distract her or himself with the abrupt orders. She gave an alarmed whimper when the craft lurched in the buffeting wind and grabbed the webbing behind the seat to keep from being flung around.

"BP one hundred over sixty-five," she reported through chattering teeth.

Luke muttered a curse and a quick look in his

direction told her he was clenching his teeth. His face gleamed green and wet in the instrument lights as he battled to keep them from being blown into the tree line. Lilah wondered if it was sweat or rain slicking his skin and decided it was most likely a mixture of both. Heck, she'd broken out in a cold sweat herself the moment she'd known they were flying out.

Blinking to clear her swimming vision, she ordered herself to get a grip. He seemed in control of things but considering the way he'd reacted that afternoon, she wondered if he was really okay to get them back safely without having a flashback, a panic attack or whatever it was he'd had.

To her vast relief he managed to stabilize the chopper and the next second they rose sharply, leaving Lilah's belly behind along with her notion of being in control. She was literally putting her life in the hands of a man who'd crashed his last chopper. If she survived this, she was never leaving terra firma again. Ever.

Praying that some guardian angel was watching over them, Lilah concentrated on Jeff's vitals. She briefly stopped using the resus bag to pull his lip down to check the mucous tissue for cyanosis. She couldn't really see in the dim light and reached for his hand to give the end of his finger a hard pinch. *Dammit.* It was virtually impossible to detect capillary refill either. She would just have to rely on instinct to get him through the worst and pray for the best.

Ignoring Luke's constant mutters and curses as he fought the buffeting wind, Lilah felt herself edge towards the limit of her own control, praying her perception of the endless flight into the mountains earlier had been the result of stress. Hopefully it would be mere minutes before they landed on the hospital roof.

But after what seemed like hours she noticed the water bottle had turned from a light pink to red. She must have said something because Luke's head swung towards her.

"What? What's wrong?" he demanded brusquely, breaking off to curse when he caught sight of the problem.

"I think we just went from a pneumo to a tension haemo and I won't be able to tell where the blood is coming from without opening him up."

"Pulse and BP?" he growled, and even Lilah could hear the tension in his voice.

"About one forty. His BP is dropping," Lilah answered.

"Cyanosis?"

She looked up briefly, but Luke had gone back to concentrating on the instruments. "There's not enough light to see the capillary refill but his lips are pale."

"Okay. Can you check the refrigeration unit?" Lilah abandoned the resus bag for a moment while she reached for the refrigerator. It was filled with trays of medication but no blood.

"It's empty."

Luke cursed. "Set up more Ringer's lactate but watch for haemo-dilution. You don't want his levels dropping below five." Lilah knew what would happen then. There wouldn't be enough oxygen in the diluted blood and his organs would start shutting down.

With shaking hands, she attached another bag and felt for his pulse, detecting arrhythmia in his tachycardia. Her pulse spiked with alarm and she opened her mouth to report it just as light flashed, illuminating the interior like someone had switched on the sun. Almost instantly there was an earsplitting explosion.

The sound engulfed the small aircraft, making it shudder and rattle as it was tossed through the air like a flimsy toy rather than a few thousand pounds of metal. Over the shriek of the engine and the booming echo reverberating through the mountains, Lilah heard herself scream.

"Luke," she yelled, and if he heard her through the headset he gave no indication. Posture tense, the muscles in his shoulders strained, threatening the seams of his shirt. He clearly had better things to do than reassure her they were okay. Lilah hoped that wasn't an omen.

Light flashed again, but this time it was further away and the booming response echoed around them. "Luke," she yelled again, scarcely aware that she was crying until she swiped irritably at the wetness on her cheeks. Her heart was pounding faster than Jeff's and she felt lightheaded. "*Dammit*, what's wrong?"

His muttered curse reached her over the terrible noise and out the corner of her eye she saw him wrestle the pitch lever as though it was alive and determined to defy him.

A quick glance at Jeff told her he was in serious trouble. Even in the dim light she could see that his skin was gray and clammy, and blood trickled from one corner of his mouth. The branch must have nicked something more serious than they'd originally thought and he was going into shock.

Then she heard "Uh-oh" through her headset and her stomach cramped violently. She squeaked, "What? What now?" and Luke sent her a quick look over his shoulder that she struggled to interpret.

His eyes were narrowed and intense and a muscle popped along his jaw. "Don't freak out," he ordered, just as the chopper lurched sideways again. "But we have a little problem."

"Problem? *Problem?* Jeff going into shock is a problem. What could be worse?" She gulped back the rising hysteria and felt more tears blur her vision. Dammit, now wasn't the time to lose it.

*Or maybe now's the perfect time to lose it.*

"The tail rotors are sluggish and the gyro-scope is all over the place."

"Wha-at?" *Okay, so that was officially worse.*

There was another blinding flash of blue-white light and she opened her mouth to scream. Searing sulfur scorching her lungs as the chopper slewed sideways, jolting violently. There was a popping sound and she realized with dawning horror that she could literally see each individual rotor blade. The chopper lurched sickeningly and dipped forward.

Lilah gave a squeak of alarm and whipped her head around to gape at him. "Seriously? *Seriously?*"

Luke ignored her, cursing a blue streak. "Hold on," he yelled, hands flying over the control panel as his knees gripped the CPL. "I've got this."

The next few seconds passed in a blur. Lilah watched, eyes locked on his face as he fought the controls, and wondered if they were about to die. It seemed they were, she realized with a gasp of horror as the chopper tilted again and began a slow, lazy spiral towards the ground. Sucking in a terrified breath, she squeezed her eyes closed and braced for impact as a raucous warning alarm filled the interior.

"Oh, God," she whimpered, and fumbled the

manual resuscitator, thinking that in a couple of seconds Jeff might not need it.

"Have a little faith, woman," Luke yelled, but his voice was tight with tension. He was worried and Lilah tried not to imagine how close they were to the ground.

Just when she thought they would slam into the mountain, he launched into a blur of motion. The craft jolted once and then shuddered. *Oh, boy.* It didn't sound good.

"C'mon, c'mon," he urged through gritted teeth, and suddenly there was a high-pitched whine and he whooped, "Gotcha!" as the rotors began to turn with a sluggish *whop, whop.*

Lilah cracked open one eye and imagined the ground rushing up to meet them despite the rotating blades. She gave a terrified squeak just as they lurched upwards, the skids slapping the tops of the trees. *Too close. Way too close.*

Then they were bumping over the canopy and she could finally exhale wondering if her heart would ever return to its normal state.

"I think the lightning fried a couple of circuits," Luke yelled over the continued blare of the warning alarm. "Maybe even struck the tail rotor."

More good news? Lilah gulped. "What…what does that mean?"

"It means we're going to have to land."

"Here?"

Luke steeled himself against the fear and tension he could hear in Lilah's voice and shook his head. In his estimation they were about a mile from the exclusive Greendale Country Club. Yep. There were the lights. He just hoped he could make the golf course without crashing into the lake. The chopper's night vision capability had been fried in that last strike and something was wrong with the terrain awareness warning system. Luke would be flying blind and the damn blaring alarm was getting on his last nerve.

Behind him, Lilah sat frozen with terror and he didn't dare take his eyes off the instruments to reassure her. He'd tried telling her to have a little faith but he suspected she'd stopped listening a while back. He couldn't blame her. This was about as scary as his last mission. At least they didn't have RPGs exploding all around them. Although the lightning had been bad enough and for a minute there he'd thought he was going to have a flashback to rival all flashbacks.

Right now he didn't have time to panic. Which was probably a good thing. He just hoped he didn't lose it until he was alone.

Bellowing instructions to the control tower over the shriek of alarms, he gave them his location and spared a moment to be grateful for his military training and experience. Somewhere

along the way he'd stopped hyperventilating and
sweating in terror and was now flying on reflex.
The black dots obscuring his vision had vanished, leaving him steady and relaxed. Well…as
relaxed as he was ever going to be while keeping them from crashing into the rocky cliffs or
the icy lake below.

The aircraft abruptly jerked once and then he
felt the ailing tail rotors clip the treetops just as
they ploughed through the last hundred feet of
thick brush.

The instant the chopper made the clearing
Luke worked the foot levers, forcing the craft
around to keep from spiraling into the ground—
or taking out the front of the building.

A muffled "What's wrong now?" was abruptly
cut off the moment the right skid clipped the
flagpole. Something broke free and the shriek
of the rotors sounded like a host of banshees
had escaped the depths of hell. Then the chopper jolted and tipped sideways.

Too close, he thought an instant before a rotor
plowed into the asphalt. In slow motion they
tipped forward and crashed nose first into the
ground with a bone-jarring force that slammed
his teeth together and sent shock waves through
his body. Lilah's cry was abruptly cut off and
all Luke could think about was that she hadn't
been strapped in.

For a moment he saw stars and, though darkness tugged at him, he fought to remain conscious. He needed to get to her...see if she was okay.

The scream of the straining engines momentarily distracted him and he paused to slam the off lever before the rotors could snap off and became lethal missiles.

For an instant there was absolute silence and then the aircraft toppled backwards in slow motion, finally coming to rest on its side. Outside, rain continued to drum against the metal fuselage and it took him a couple of moments to realize he was seeing water running off the splintered windshield, bleeding light and color into a nightmarish glow.

The utter silence inside the chopper finally nudged him into action.

"Lilah?" He reached for the harness buckle and tugged, then tugged again when it failed to open. Probably because he was hanging at an angle and his weight kept the clasp from opening.

*"Lilah!"*

Luke felt around with his feet until he could brace himself against the passenger seat and after a couple of yanks the clasp abruptly released.

Freed, he grasped the back of the seat and hauled himself upright to scramble into the rear. In the watery light from the building's security lights he saw a chaos of equipment and supplies. It took a few seconds to locate Lilah pinned against the door by the angle of the disabled chopper. She lay unmoving amidst a scattering of debris and his heart clenched at the sight of something dark and wet staining one side of her face.

Fortunately Jeff was still strapped in and the stretcher remained secured, but a glance in his direction told Luke the man was in serious trouble.

With quick economic movements he cleared the debris away from Lilah and checked for injuries but the only external sign was the steady flow of blood soaking into her hair from the head wound. He leaned closer to examine it while the fingers of his free hand located the sturdy beat of her pulse in the soft flesh just beneath her jaw.

She was alive, he thought on a rush of relief so intense it made him dizzy. After tonight she had a legitimate reason to fear flying and he tried not to feel responsible. But he didn't have time to move her or wait until she regained consciousness. He had to act fast or Jeff would slip away.

Yanking on the defibrillator, he prayed the lightning hadn't fried it since manual chest compressions would cause further damage. Unfortunately, blood in the oral cavity would make his job that much harder. If he had to perform traditional resus, with broken ribs and the intra-thorax drain, who knew what other damage he could cause to an already critical patient. One thing he knew, he had to keep the ranger's heart pumping, no matter what.

Impatiently willing the machine to charge, Luke looked around for the resus bag and spotted it a few feet away. A soft moan sounded and he turned in time to see Lilah's lashes flicker.

"Lilah, open your eyes but don't move," he ordered calmly, as she looked around in a daze.

"What?"

"We landed." Well, in a manner of speaking, he thought with a flash of humor now that her eyes were open and he was sure she wasn't going to die. He retrieved the resus bag and moved back to the stretcher. "Don't move until you've done a full body check." After a couple of seconds he looked her way. "Are you okay?"

"My head hurts."

"Is that all?"

"Nothing's broken, if that's what you mean. But my head *really* hurts."

"I'll check it out later." He sent her a quick look as she struggled upright, a shaking hand going to her head. "Right now you're lucid and that's the important thing."

"How's Jeff?"

"I'm going to have to defib. Are you up to giving me a hand?"

"I...I think so. Give me a minute."

"He doesn't have a minute. The defibrillator is nearly charged and I need you to hold the bag."

He was conscious of Lilah shuffling closer and resisted the urge to take her in his arms. He knew she was hurting and probably not just her head, but she was being a real trooper. Frankly, the best thing he could do for her was keep her too busy to go into shock. Besides, they had to keep Jeff alive long enough for the ambulance crew to arrive.

He gave her trembling fingers a quick hang-in-there squeeze as he passed over the resus bag. Then, moving quickly, he stripped off the space blanket and positioned the paddles, waiting impatiently for the high-pitched sound to signal the charge.

When it sounded, he said, "Clear." There was a sharp jolt and Jeff's body momentarily arched upwards before flopping back onto the stretcher like a rag doll. "Again." This time the jolt was weaker and Jeff barely responded. Luke moved to reset the machine and noticed the green light abruptly die. He tried it again. Nothing.

He cursed and fiddled with the power switch. "There goes the power," he said, glancing at Lilah. She still looked a little dazed and seemed oblivious to the blood trickling down her face.

She nodded and resumed using the resus bag. "So we do it manually." Her face was ghost white in the stingy light but at least she was responsive and rational, although he suspected she was drawing on sheer willpower.

"See if you can find some atropine. I think I saw some in the case," he growled, beginning CPR while taking care not to exert too much force on Jeff's ribs.

Lilah located the case, quickly preparing and administering the drug while Luke checked BP.

"Sixty over forty. It's dropping," he said brusquely. "Whatever you do, keep that up. *Dammit, where are they?*"

"Do you think they got the message?"

Luke didn't know so he started praying and just as he was beginning to think the ambulance wasn't coming, he heard the siren wail over the drumming rain and heaved a sigh of relief. Within seconds, flashing lights filled the interior and paramedics were crawling inside, brushing them aside.

Luke told them who he was and shot off rapid-fire instructions as the crew disappeared with the stretcher. When they were gone he turned to find Lilah slumped against the fuselage, her head tilted forward onto her drawn-up knees. The fall of hair hid her face from view. Her arms were wrapped around her shins and even with the rain pinging off the metal he could hear her teeth chattering like a pair of wind-up dentures.

Moving closer he noticed for the first time that she was shivering so hard her whole body shook.

"Lilah."

As though realizing she was under scrutiny, Lilah stilled and Luke could literally feel the tension pumping off her body.

Without looking up, she mumbled something he couldn't hear so he moved to sit beside her and gently bumped her shoulder. "Hey, look on the bright side."

Her voice hitched. "There's a bright side?"

"We made it in one piece."

He'd meant to lighten her mood but when she gave a strangled sob and turned towards him, he opened his arms. She burrowed close and pressed her face into his neck, the move making him aware of the myriad aches he hadn't noticed until now. Now that the adrenalin was fading, he was feeling a bit shaky himself.

He dropped his face into her hair and tightened his grip, sending up a prayer of thanks for their narrow escape.

For long moments they stayed that way until a voice enquired, "You folks need help?" and Luke looked up to see two expectant faces peering through the doorway at them.

"I thought you guys left," he said, pulling Lilah closer as though he thought they might snatch her away. That instinctive move made him pause but then he decided it was probably just reaction from having survived possible death together.

"They didn't know what we would find so they sent two wagons," the paramedic said, gesturing to the crumpled metal and scattered equipment. "You two are damn lucky to be alive."

Luke gave a strangled snort at the understatement and drew in a shaky breath. He didn't need anyone to tell him how close it had been.

"We might as well take you back to County Gen to get checked out," the paramedic continued. "Shock has a way of masking internal injuries."

Lilah couldn't stop shivering. She felt icy to the core even though Luke had wrapped a blanket around her before examining her head wound.

They were in the back of the ambulance as it sped through the night and the scene was so normal—except for her being the patient, of course—that everything that had happened that night seemed like a surreal nightmare. It was creepy and weird.

Luke held up his hand. "How many fingers?"

Lilah squinted against the pain. "Twenty," she murmured, feeling weary beyond belief. Intellectually she knew she was in shock but it didn't help that her skull felt like it wanted to explode.

Just moving her head caused excruciating pain to arrow through her skull and her neck felt as if one wrong move would cause it to shatter. Heck, her entire body felt as though it would shatter.

"Yeah, right," Luke growled, ruffling his already tousled hair with his fingers and Lilah had an overwhelming urge to lift a hand and smooth the silky strands. But moving required effort and she just didn't have the energy to do anything more strenuous than breathe.

"I just need a couple of painkillers," she lied. "I'm fine. Really. It's Jeff I'm worried about. And you."

Luke turned to stare at her. "Me? Why me?"

She gave a small smile and managed to lift a hand to his face. His shadowed jaw felt bristly beneath her fingertips and she shivered at the unexpected sensuality of it. It reminded her of the hours he'd spent exploring her naked body—God, had it been just a few hours ago?

"We kind of crashed. I was worried it would bring back bad memories. Of the last time you flew, I mean."

Luke looked momentarily taken aback then his expression turned thoughtful. "Actually...I think it helped me get over myself. In a hair-of-the-dog kinda way."

Lilah studied him closely. "Really?" she asked skeptically. "I got a quick look at the chopper before you closed the ambulance doors. It looked pretty mangled."

Luke drew a gentle finger along the line of her jaw towards her mouth. The expression in his gaze made her pulse leap and her skin tingle. "I'm just glad you're not."

And then he did something that made the backs of her eyes sting and she had to bite her lip to keep from giving in to the tears that had been threatening for what seemed like years. He ran gentle hands over her body as though to re-assure himself that she was indeed in one piece and then carefully drew her into his arms.

She went willingly, welcoming his strength and heat. Welcoming the strong, steady beat of his heart. She wrapped her arms around him and clung.

"Rest now," he murmured into her hair. "I've got you."

# CHAPTER TEN

LILAH TURNED THE key again and listened to the ominous click of the engine with growing disbelief. *No, no, no,* she begged silently. *Not now.* It had been a really long week and an even longer shift and she didn't have the energy to face another crisis. *Especially not now, dammit.*

Not when she was feeling fragile and exhausted. Not when she just wanted to go home, climb into bed and pull the covers up over her head so she could hide from the world.

Resisting the urge to drop her forehead onto the steering-wheel and bawl, Lilah gritted her teeth and reached beneath the dash to pop the hood. Besides, weeping never did anyone any good. It clogged the sinuses and made your eyes red and swollen, which was the last thing in attractive. But then again, looking beneath the hood wouldn't do any good either, but at least it felt proactive.

Slowly inhaling, she got out of the car, fiddled around until she found the catch, and lifted the hood. She propped it up and stared into the engine, waiting for divine guidance.

When none came she sighed and went back to lean in through the open door and dig around in her shoulder bag for her cellphone. Only it was as dead as the car. Obviously she'd forgotten to charge it. Again.

*Great. Just great.* What else could go wrong?

Unbidden, tears pricked her eyes, and her throat ached. It made her wonder what the heck was wrong with her. She wasn't normally this… emotional. She'd handled crises before but now all she wanted to do was curl up in a tight ball and cry like a little kid.

Sniffing, she tossed the phone onto the passenger seat, slammed the door and went back round to peer into the engine. Only thing was, nothing appeared broken—which meant she'd have to go back inside and call for a cab.

But that required too much effort, so she sank back against the car with a sigh of defeat and slid to the ground. With one leg tucked against her butt, she propped her elbow on her knee, shoved her fingers in her hair and squeezed her eyes shut.

God, she was tired. She hadn't had a decent night's sleep since…since…okay, so she didn't want to think about her night with Luke. Or the crash. If she did she might start bawling for real. And she didn't want to think about her earlier run-in with her boss either. He was a jerk and once she started, she probably wouldn't stop until she'd cried about everything that had happened since her mother's death.

She was so wrapped up in her own misery she didn't hear anyone approach until a deep voice said, "Problem?" somewhere overhead. Lilah gave a silent groan. *Why me?* she demanded silently, wishing the earth would open up and swallow her.

She considered pretending to be invisible, but she didn't think Luke would take the hint and go away. He'd been amazingly protective since… since that night and she was worried that she would cling and weep all over him.

It was embarrassing. She'd done enough clinging the night of the crash and wanted to forget the whole thing. Besides, his behavior had most likely been the result of them having survived a harrowing experience together. She would be smart not to read anything into it. That way lay disaster…and heartbreak. At least for her, she reminded herself.

She felt the air change and cracked open one eye to see him crouched at her side. The dim light illuminated half his face, leaving the other in deep shadow. It was frightening how much she liked looking at him.

"What makes you think I have a problem?" she slurred, feeling punch drunk with fatigue.

A smile tugged the corner of his mouth not in shadow and he lifted a hand to gently brush a few escapee curls off her face.

"Maybe because you're sitting on the ground beside your car looking kind of pathetic and I feel sorry for you."

Lilah might look pathetic—heck, she felt pathetic—but she didn't need anyone feeling sorry for her. She was doing enough of that herself. She opened her eyes all the way, knocked his hand away and made to stand up, but he gently pushed her back until her butt hit the concrete.

"Stay there while I check your car," he murmured softly, and rose in one effortless move that she might have envied if she wasn't so exhausted.

Of course he knew about cars. He was the kind of man who knew everything and was probably good at it too. *Yep. Even taking a girl to heaven.* The only thing he was really bad at was commitment. He'd told her a little about his childhood the night of the storm, including his determination to never repeat his parents' mistakes. Heck, she could empathize. She was into avoiding bad history herself.

She must have dozed a little because the next thing she knew he was crouching at her side again and running his thumb across her jaw. She blinked up into his face, momentarily confused.

"Wha—?"

"Come on, Sleeping Beauty," he said, closing his hands around her upper arms. "I'm taking you home." When he rose to his feet he drew her up with him and Lilah swayed dizzily for a moment before stepping away from his warm strength.

The urge to cling was still way too strong.

"It's okay," she said, when what she really wanted was to lay her head on his chest and listen to the strong beat of his heart. "I'll call a cab."

"It's almost midnight." His voice was rife with exasperation as he folded his arms across his wide chest and looked at her like she was being irrational. Heck irrational was becoming her middle name. "It could take a while."

"I'm fine, really," she said, turning away to peer at the engine. "So what's wrong with her?"

"Her?" His amused voice was so close that her body heated from neck to thigh as he looked over her shoulder. Shivering, Lilah rubbed at the goose bumps dotting her arms and looked up into his shadowed face. Her breath caught.

*God, he was hotter than high noon in Bogota.* And just as dangerous.

Which was so not good, *dammit*, she thought when her nerve endings tingled and something hot settled low and deep in her belly. *Dumb, dumb, dumb.*

She turned away to glare into the damn engine.

"Do you know what's wrong?"

"You're exhausted."

"Not me, the car."

"The battery is dead and the starter's fried."
*Yeah, she'd kind of figured that.* "So I take it I won't be driving home tonight?"

"Yes, you will," Luke said, nudging her aside so he could close the hood. "With me." Without waiting for her permission, he retrieved her keys, dead cellphone, light jacket and shoulder bag and locked the car. "Come on, you look like you need about twelve hours' sleep."

Lilah snatched her belongings from him and stomped away, unaccountably annoyed because he was telling her—subtly—that she looked like crap.

He caught up with her easily and with a firm hand curled around her upper arm steered her away from the hospital entrance towards a big black bike parked at the end of the row. *Figured he would ride a sexy badass bike.*

Infuriated with his high-handed manhandling—and her own rioting emotions—Lilah yanked at her arm, muttering irritably about arrogant, cocky alpha males.

"What was that?" he asked, and something in his voice made her turn to catch him fighting a smile. She barely resisted the urge to punch his amazing mouth.

"I said you have no idea what I need," she

muttered. Actually, neither did she, which might explain her moodiness. And then his eyes turned hot and she sucked in a sharp breath and stumbled back a couple steps.

*Holy mother of— No!* She didn't need *that*, she assured herself, and hastily backed up again. She needed to be alone. She needed... Luke yanked her against him and before she could demand to know what he was doing he'd caught her mouth in a kiss tainted with wild anger and desperate need.

At first Lilah was too stunned to do anything except withstand the heated assault but after a couple beats her bones began to melt. She fought the sensations but her body took over, swaying closer, and her palms slid up his hard chest despite her determination to keep them stiffly at her sides. By degrees, her mouth softened until it clung to the sculpted lines of his. *God, he tasted good. Like furious masculine need and... dark sin.*

Against her mouth he growled, "Dammit," in between bites and a light suction that made her senses swim. "I didn't want to do this...don't want this."

His words took a couple of seconds to register and when they did Lilah shoved back, feeling unaccountably wounded. She gave him the sharp edge of her shoulder and out the corner of her eye she caught sight of a muscle twitching in his hard jaw as though he was barely holding himself in check.

*Good. At least she wasn't the only one struggling with control issues.*

Turning to glare daggers at him, Lilah deliberately wiped the back of her hand across her mouth as though to erase the feel and taste of him. *Right, as if.*

Stung by his words as much as his manner, she demanded, "Why are you here, then?"

Luke sighed, planted his big hands on his hips and narrowed his eyes as though she made his head hurt. Considering the unexpected blow to her heart, that made them even.

"Someone has to look out for you."

"Don't be ridiculous," she snapped, and swung away to hide the raw hurt in her eyes. "I can take care of myself." She'd been taking care of herself a long time and was tired of doing everything alone.

She lifted a hand to rub at the ache in her chest.

"Sure you can," he growled, interrupting her pity party. "That's why I find you sitting on the floor of a parking garage at midnight with your car and cell batteries dead. That's why I… Are you crying?"

"Don't flatter yourself." She wasn't, she assured herself, swiping at the scalding tears with her arm. She was just so…so…mad. Mad at him.

Mad at herself. Mad at the world. She sniffed and her eyes swam again. *Dammit.*

"C'm'ere," Luke growled, yanking her against him in a move that was more irritable than caring. But when she stiffened and tried to shove him away, he tightened his arms and dropped his chin on her head. The effort of keeping everything together until she was alone was too much and with a strangled sob Lilah buried her face against him as hot tears finally erupted, instantly soaking the soft, warm fabric of his shirt.

She didn't know how long he stood in the dim parking garage simply holding her as she cried about stuff that didn't even make any sense.

Finally, when the storm of weeping passed, she discovered she'd burrowed as close as she could to his warm strength and was gripping his T-shirt with both hands—as though to keep him from escaping. But his big arms had trapped her close as though he didn't intend letting her go any time soon.

She was fine with that. *Really.* She kind of liked the feel of him against her. She liked the sound of his heart thudding beneath her ear and the warm smell of man making her senses swim. It was comforting and kind of…relaxing.

But she'd be fine in a minute.

"Bad day?" His voice rumbled in her ear and sent warm little vibrations zinging through her body. She burrowed even closer and nodded.

"Wanna talk about it?" His big warm hand smoothed a path of comfort from the back of her head down the length of her spine and up again. Lilah quickly shook her head. She really didn't. She wanted to continue standing there wrapped in his arms, feeling warm and safe. She wanted to pretend this was real and not just some hot guy feeling sorry for her because she was a mess.

After a moment Luke loosened his hold and gently put a few inches between them. Cool air rushed over Lilah and she shivered at the abrupt withdrawal of his heat. Ducking her head, she sucked in air, totally embarrassed by her emotional outburst.

She wasn't normally this needy.

"Let's get you home," he growled, sliding his hand down her back to her waist, urging her in the direction of his motorbike. His voice had been deep and rough with suppressed emotion but when Lilah sneaked a peek his face was impassive.

"When last did you eat something?" he asked, opening a side compartment on the bike to remove a spare helmet. Lilah couldn't remember but shook her head before drying her wet cheek on her shoulder. Her stomach revolted at the thought of food.

"I'm not hungry." She took the helmet from him and watched as he pulled on a huge leather jacket. It reminded her of the one she still had in her hallway closet.

"You ever been on one of these?" he asked, zipping up the front with long, tanned fingers. Lilah shook her head, too absorbed—and maybe a little intimidated—by the badass picture he made dressed in black leather, biker boots and well-worn jeans. She shivered—and not just because she was cold.

Pausing, Luke stared at her like she'd just admitted to something indecent. "You're kidding, right?"

She didn't know why she flushed. Guys in black leather had never appealed to her before. Especially not guys radiating sex appeal and testosterone from a hundred paces.

His mouth curled into a wicked smile and his eyes twinkled. "I'd have thought a girl like you would be used to being on the back of some hog with a bad boy."

Lilah narrowed her gaze and stood with one knee bent and her fists on her hips. "A girl like me?"

Luke laughed and fisted the front of her T to yank her against him before dropping a hard, hot kiss on her sulky mouth. "Don't get all bent out of shape, Wild Woman," he grinned, taking the helmet from her nerveless fingers. "I only meant girls who look like you always have a long line of bad boys lined up to take them for a wild ride around town."

Lilah stared at him open-mouthed, knowing he was suggesting something a lot more X-rated than a mere ride around town. "You're kidding, right?"

"Nope. In fact..." he tugged an escaped curl "...I can just picture you flipping all these wild curls over your shoulder and fluttering those hell-smoke eyes at some poor dumb sap. I bet you were beautiful and offhand, leaving a trail of broken hearts."

Lilah snorted at the ridiculous picture he painted. "I was plain and way too serious," she informed him. "Guys don't go for plain, nerdy redheads."

Luke shook his head as though she was deluding herself. "Don't kid yourself. There's nothing plain about you. You're a study in rose, gold and cream and you hide all that simmering passion behind those smoky eyes and neat outfits. It's a wonder you don't combust with all that suppressed emotion."

He shoved the helmet down over her head and all Lilah could think was, *Simmering passion? Me?*

She flipped up the visor to scowl at him. "My mother warned me about boys like you," she said primly, snatching her jacket from him and growling when he laughed because he was as far from a boy as he could get and still carry similar DNA.

"Your mother's a smart woman." He pulled on his own helmet and swung his long leg over the bike to settle on the padded seat. Kicking up the bike stand, he shoved up his visor and the grin he aimed her way was as wicked as his gaze. "But don't worry, wild thing. You're safe with me," he drawled an instant before the bike started with a throaty roar.

*No, she wasn't*, Lilah thought. *Not really. And certainly not in the way he implied.* But she must be a wild woman because the next thing she knew she was climbing up behind him and placing her hands on his waist. She nearly moaned when his muscles shifted as he turned his head, reminding her of their wild night in a wild storm. His green eyes caught and held hers and Lilah shivered at the heat in them.

"Put your arms around me, wild thing," Luke crooned, his voice all low and rough and wickedly suggestive. "And hold on tight."

For a long heated moment they stared at each other until Lilah could scarcely breathe. She was fighting an overwhelming impulse to escape. Or to hold on as tight as she could. And never let go.

Spooked by her thoughts and the simmering intensity suddenly crackling in the air around them, Lilah flipped the visor closed and gingerly wrapped her arms around his hard body as though he were a live grenade.

For a moment longer Luke's gaze remained on her until he revved the engine and finally turned away to take off towards the exit ramp. By the time the cool mountain air brushed her body she was plastered against his back as though she wanted to be part of him. She could feel every move and muscle twitch from her knees to her shoulders. Every part that was fused to him tingled and melted in the heat pumping off him like a nuclear reactor. It was kind of embarrassing just how much she tingled and melted in places he'd awakened from permafrost just nine days ago.

Embarrassing and exhilarating.

Once they left the city limits and hit the road leading up through the mountains around the lake Luke opened up the engine and Lilah squeezed her eyes closed and pressed closer. Fortunately the roads were quiet as they zipped along the winding road. And each time he shifted, leaning into the curves, she moved and shifted with him.

Sucking in a shaky breath, Lilah wondered if she was imagining the rising heat and excitement. But then laughter rumbled through him and she knew he was doing it deliberately. Deliberately making her press closer. Deliberately making her tighten her arms and grip his narrow hips and thighs with hers in an attempt to keep from flying off into the darkness.

He was a danger to women everywhere and he knew it. But for some reason she couldn't be mad. Despite the terror of whipping through the night at breakneck speed, she was enjoying the hard powerful feel of him against her and wondered at the bubbles of terrified excitement popping in her veins.

She knew the instant they entered the older, more shabbily genteel suburb of Greenstone Park, where she'd grown up. Luke slowed and geared down to make a couple of turns and Lilah lifted her head to give him directions but he was already turning into her driveway and bringing the bike to a stop.

For an insane moment she didn't want to move, didn't want to let him go. But that was ridiculous. She was fine. She didn't need anyone, especially someone like him. Besides, he most likely had plans of his own and couldn't wait to dump her on her doorstep.

By the time he killed the engine and released the bike stand Lilah had loosened her death grip around his waist. She used his wide shoulders to help with balance as she dismounted, grateful for the hand he shot out when her knees wobbled. She pulled off the helmet and looked up to find his features in deep shadow.

"You could have killed us," she huffed, thrusting the helmet at his belly, but all he did was grin and toss it into a side compartment.

"Please," he snorted, raking a hand through his tousled hair. "I'm an expert."

Lilah snorted her opinion of his delusional statement and rooted around in her shoulder bag for her house keys. "Thanks for the lift," she began, then halted abruptly when she realized he'd gone ahead and was leaning casually against the pillar holding up her porch. He looked big and sinfully dangerous in the dark and she shivered—a good and bad kind of shiver. One that stole her breath, tightened her nipples and clenched the muscles in her thighs. Definitely bad, but it felt *so-o-o* good.

"What are you doing?" Her voice emerged all breathless and panicky.

"Waiting," he drawled quietly, and the rough, sexy sound reached out and stroked over her flesh, drawing her towards him, stealing her will to resist.

"For what?"

His teeth gleamed white in the darkness as he chuckled. "Coffee?"

Lilah gulped and fiddled with the strap of her purse. "What if I don't have coffee?" she squeaked breathlessly. "What if I want to be alone?"

He chuckled again, dark and velvet soft, before reaching out to grab the front of her jacket.

He reeled her in slowly and the glitter in his eyes made her suck in a sharp, excited breath.

She let out a soft "Oomph" as her body thudded against his.

He leaned down to murmur, "Do you want to be alone?" in her ear. Hot shivers raced over Lilah's skin, leaving behind a chaos of sensation and goose bumps.

*Holy cow, the man was lethal.*

She knew she needed to take a step back but the instant she looked up past his square jaw to his sculpted lips she couldn't move. Her senses swam and a dangerous lassitude invaded her limbs. She wanted that mouth on her more than she wanted sleep.

"No. *Yes*," she gulped, planting her palms against his chest and attempting to wedge a little space between them so she could breathe without inhaling the potent mix of testosterone and pheromones that never failed to steal her mind.

"No? Or yes?"

"Um…"

His chuckle was deliciously deep, as though he knew what he was doing to her. "Why don't I help you make up your mind, wild thing?" he murmured against her throat, before sucking the delicate skin into his mouth. Sensation, hot, liquid and exciting, shot into every nerve ending and Lilah abruptly became light-headed.

"I…um…" she stammered on a shaky sigh. "I don't think—"

"Good," he growled, snatching the keys from her grasp as he nipped her ear lobe and slipped his hand beneath her little tank, his warm, rough palm scraping already painfully sensitive nerve endings. "Don't think. Just feel."

He one-handedly inserted the key into the lock and the next thing he was dragging her inside and kicking the door shut. Feeling a little dazed, Lilah swayed and then she was being shoved back against the door as Luke took her mouth with barely controlled violence. As though the tight leash he'd had on his emotions had suddenly snapped.

"I thought you didn't want to do this?" she moaned against his mouth.

"That's the problem," he muttered, nipping at her lips. "I do." Taking advantage of her gasp, his tongue invaded her mouth, the wildly exciting masculine impatience frying all her mental circuits. She could almost hear the snap and sizzle as each IQ point fizzled out beneath the heated onslaught. And when he abandoned her lips to streak a line of fire down her throat and tease a thumb over her tight nipple, Lilah gave a long, low moan and arched into his hands.

She blinked against the light exploding behind her eyelids. "I thought…I thought you wanted coffee," she gasped, fisting his soft, dark hair as his big hands closed over her lace-covered breasts.

Luke bit her neck and then sucked her abused flesh into his hot mouth, making her shudder with excitement. "I don't need coffee," he growled, tightening his grasp and returning to her mouth, where he peppered her lips with teasing nips until she growled in frustration and tried to bite him.

His chuckle was dark as sin.

"What...do...you...need?" Lilah panted, locking her shaky knees at what he clearly had in mind.

Without replying, Luke released her, retreating a couple of feet to stand breathing heavily in the dark. For one awful moment she thought he was backing off. But then he planted a shoulder in her middle and the next thing she was upside down as he jogged up the stairs.

She gave a shocked "*Oomph*" and made a grab for his shirt in an attempt to hold on but encountered smooth, warm skin instead. Momentarily distracted, she let her free hand touch all that yummy hard flesh until a sharp slap on her bottom got her attention.

"Bedroom?" Luke rumbled, and Lilah barely managed to squeak out a reply. The next minute she was flying through the air. She landed with a bounce and a giggle, all the exhaustion and trauma of the past few weeks wiped out by his playful mood.

The air stirred and after a brief pause soft light spilled from the bedside lamp, driving back the darkness. Lilah's breath caught. While most of him was still in darkness, lamplight revealed a portion of Luke's rock-hard abs, his long jeans-clad legs and the impressive bulge behind his zipper. Her pulse lurched drunkenly at the sight. He was hugely aroused, the thick shaft clearly visible beneath the soft, worn denim.

Her breath escaped in a loud whoosh as her avid gaze ate up the vision of masculine perfection standing over her. Then he reached for his zipper and before Lilah had looked her fill he was shoving his jeans and underwear down his legs and reaching for her sneakers. Within seconds he'd stripped her naked and joined her on the bed, his big body enveloping her in delicious heat.

For a couple of beats she blinked up at him, panting like she'd been the one to jog up the stairs carrying a hundred pounds over her shoulder. He was hot and hard against her and Lilah shifted languorously, enjoying the sensation of skin on skin and the anticipation of what was to come. A growl rumbled in his chest and his eyes, sleepy and aroused, burned like green fire.

Lilah's pulse gave a little bump of fear and excitement. The excitement was a no-brainer but the fear was new. Wild, uncontrolled emotions were racing through her, making her hyperaware of every inch of skin-on-skin contact. They were so sharp and painfully intense that a little voice at the back of her mind urged her to run—escape while she still could.

Her body tensed and her heart thundered as she prepared to obey but then—as if he could read her intent—Luke thrust long fingers into her messy curls. Holding her in place, he lowered his head and nipped at her chin.

"I have you trapped, wild thing," he rasped against her flesh. "There's no escape."

"There...there's not?"

He shook his head and dragged his mouth to her ear. "You had your chance."

And Lilah thought, *No, I never stood a chance.* Not against this. Not against the green eyes that were sometimes bright with arousal or laughter, or dark and brooding. And certainly not against the intense pull of his aura on hers.

Then his teeth nipped at her lobe and she gave a full-body shudder, all thoughts of secrets extinguished. Her nipples tightened into aching points and her belly clenched with a deep, aching hunger.

As if he knew what was happening to her, he rasped out, "Now it's mine."

"Y-yours?"

"And I'm ravenous." He opened his mouth

over the delicate skin of her throat and sucked it into his mouth, making her moan and shift against him. His fingers tightened against her scalp as though he expected her to bolt. "And I know just where to start."

But the last thing Lilah wanted to do was escape. Not when she ached to touch him. Not when she wanted to experience again the heated rush of anticipation as his mouth moved up to meet hers and his hands greedily claimed her body. She smoothed her palms over his hot, damp skin and arched into his rough touch, her hidden places clenching in wild anticipation. Oh God, yes!

Dragging his mouth over her skin, Luke teased her with barely there kisses until she was breathless and eager for the taste of him. Fisting her hands in his hair, she nipped his lips once, then again.

"Kiss me," she ordered huskily, and with a savage curse he did.

# CHAPTER ELEVEN

LILAH STARED INTO the steaming coffee she was stirring and ignored the greasy donut at her elbow along with the discussion going on around her. Her mind was a chaos of panicked thoughts and erotic images of the past month. Ever since Luke had moved in with her, in fact. And she was only vaguely aware of Angie filling Jenna in on all the gossip she'd missed.

Since she'd already heard it all, Lilah had lapsed into her own thoughts. Thoughts that seemed to find their way to the same place, no matter how hard she tried to think of something—anything—else. Thoughts of disasters and history repeating itself.

*And, boy, was her current disaster a doozy.*

Not that she was ready to share the details with anyone. At least not until she'd stopped hyperventilating and come to terms with it herself. *If she ever did.* But, frankly, she'd never considered *this*—mostly because she'd always been so careful never to make the same mistakes as her mother.

*Hey, Mom, look at me now!*

Like an idiot, she'd excused her fatigue, emotional vulnerability and lack of appetite on the lingering effects of the crash and long shifts at the hospital. And when Luke had asked if she was okay she'd told him she sometimes reacted to stress with an upset stomach.

*Boy, had she been wrong.*

Fortunately he'd already left this morning when the scent of the coffee he'd placed beside her bed had sent her scrambling for the bathroom. Once her stomach had stopped heaving she'd rushed out to the nearest pharmacy and bought a few early detection kits. Unfortunately HCG levels didn't lie. Little pink lines didn't lie.

At least, not five sets of them.

She was pregnant. And when she counted back she realized it had been well over two months since her last period, more than a month since the crash and…and almost four weeks since the night her car wouldn't start. Nearly four weeks since that wild mountain ride.

And not once during all that time had they forgotten to use a condom. Except…*yikes*…except for that one time at the ranger's chalet after she'd treated his snake bite. Besides, she was still supposed to be protected by her IUD—which was why she hadn't worried. *Dammit.* Which wouldn't be a problem if the father of her baby wasn't allergic to commitment...or children.

She really didn't want to think about his reaction to her news. It brought back memories she'd rather not deal with.

Besides, Luke wasn't a permanent kind of guy. He'd told her that after ten years in the military he'd only taken the job to ease back into civilian life before deciding what he wanted to do. He'd said nothing about a future with her and when she'd tried to tell him the other night that she understood "this" was a temporary thing, he hadn't disagreed.

Lilah wasn't stupid. She could read between the lines. He didn't need to tell her he had "Temporary: enjoy while you can" stamped on his sexy butt and that all he was looking for was a wild welcome-back-to-civilian-life fling.

She sighed gloomily. *Some fling!*

Besides, he owned a motorbike, for goodness' sake, and everyone knew that guys who owned motorbikes—especially ones that big—weren't the settling-down kind. They were ready to hit the road when the mood struck. They were ready to take the next available babe on a terrifyingly exhilarating mountain ride before stripping her naked, tossing her down onto the nearest bed and showing her heaven. And if the thought of him doing what he'd done to her with some other woman made Lilah's belly cramp, she blamed

it on the smell of greasy donuts and her fragile
stomach.

Frankly, she wasn't ready for more than a
fling either, but things had kind of ambushed
her and she no longer had a choice. Oh, she knew
there *were* choices she could make—if she were
so inclined. She wasn't. Wouldn't *ever* be, in
fact. And despite the inherent difficulties, the
more she thought about it, the more she realized
how much she wanted this baby.

She shivered and placed a hand over her belly.

Luke's baby.

Unfortunately, she had to face the fact that
he didn't want children. Or maybe he just didn't
want children with *her*? Lilah sucked in a sharp
breath. *Jeez. That* was something she hadn't
considered.

And she would later. Maybe.

Her breath escaped on a whoosh.

Right now her emotions were all over the
place and she was smiling one minute and on the
verge of tears the next. The last thing she wanted
to think about was her crappy past. Clearly, the
best thing she could do was concentrate on her
future—a future that would most likely com-
prise only her and her child.

*Oh, boy.*

"I leave for a few weeks and you get yourself
into all sorts of trouble."

*What?* Lilah jolted, slopping hot coffee over

the top of the disposable cup and scalding her hand. Yelping, she quickly sucked at the abused flesh before darting her startled gaze between her friends.

"What?" Had she spoken her thoughts aloud? More importantly, had she said anything revealing? Both Jenna and Angie were staring at her with the kind of look someone gave when you were about to be carted off to the loony ward. *Yeesh.* "Are you talking to me?"

Jenna leaned close and laid a hand on Lilah's arm. "Honey, are you all right?" she asked, sweetly concerned. "That's the fifth time you've sighed in the past two minutes."

"Yeah, and you've been stirring that coffee for at least ten. And what's with all the frowning, head shakes and blowing out air like you're a leaky inner tube? It's disturbing. It's like you're arguing with yourself in your head."

"That's…that's ridiculous," Lilah spluttered, and hurriedly thought up a believable lie. "I'm just worried about Jeff, that's all."

"Jeff? Who's Jeff?" Jenna demanded. "A new boyfriend? I thought Luke—"

"He's a patient," Lilah said quickly, and because she needed something to occupy her hands she picked up the donut and began ripping off pieces. "He's…um… I mean I thought he was doing better but he contracted another infection."

She knew she was babbling but she desperately needed to divert their attention away from the soap opera that was her life. She wasn't ready to discuss her…um, problem, mainly because there wasn't anything to discuss. Not yet, anyway. Besides, a few wild nights did not make a relationship, let alone an affair, even with a little complication eight months or so away.

"But enough about me." She grasped desperately at the first thing that came to mind. "Look at you. You're positively glowing. That must have been some honeymoon."

"It was *the* most fabulous honeymoon ever," Jenna agreed dreamily, and Lilah's breath whooshed out softly at having dodged a bullet. "It was…awesome." Jenna's mouth curved. "And so was he."

"Fine, rub it in," Angie snapped, pointing her half-eaten pastry at her. "Lilah's right. You do look disgustingly glowy."

Jenna waved aside their jealousy. "You have good reason to be envious, girls. But I fail to see what it has that to do with Lilah's sighing."

"It doesn't," Angie snorted. "She's annoyed that you're getting some and she's taking it out on her donut." She turned to Lilah with narrow-eyed speculation that was a little alarming. "Aren't you?"

Lilah froze. Angie was staring at her as though waiting for her to come clean about some

deep, dark secret. *Hoo, boy*, she thought hysterically. *She knows. How does she know?* Her face
heated beneath the scrutiny.

"I...uh... What was the question again?"

"Huh," Angie huffed, as though Lilah had just
confirmed her suspicions. She studied Lilah silently over the top of her disposable cup for a
couple of beats before adding almost conversa-
tionally, "Now that I think about it, you've been
like this for a while."

Jenna perked up, as though sensing juicy gossip. "Like what?" she and Lilah demanded at
the same time.

"Distracted, goofy smile, frowning, sighing
all the time." Angie ignored Lilah and addressed
Jenna. "It's sickening."

Jenna frowned. "It is?"

"Yep. Just like you were with Greg." They
both turned to stare at Lilah.

"Omigod," Jenna gasped. "She's in love."

*"Wha-a-at?"* Lilah practically shrieked, and
sat up so fast her coffee went flying all over the
mutilated donut. *"No!* Don't be ridiculous," she
said with a strained laugh, and grabbed a wad
of paper napkins as she swung her gaze frantically between her two friends. She shook her
head forcefully and blustered, "That's just...*ridiculous.*"

*Wasn't it?*

*Sure it is*, she scoffed silently, mopping up a

soggy mess. They'd only known each other a short time and…and he was leaving. Her shoulders sagged. Besides, he was from a prominent family and she'd learnt the hard way that girls like her didn't have happily-ever-afters with guys like him. Falling in love with Luke would be stupid…and…*and, God*, so darn inevitable.

She deflated like an inner tube just as several people entered the cafeteria.

The hair on Lilah's neck rose in warning. She looked up and caught sight of tousled coffee-colored hair—hair she'd had her hands in a little over twelve hours ago—a familiar broad back and…*uh-oh*…her nipples tightened.

She sucked in a startled breath and had to clench her thighs together to stop her body's visceral response from becoming public knowledge. *Holy bejeezers, this is getting out of hand,* she told herself. *And exactly what got you knocked up in the first place.*

A blush crept into her face and she didn't know whether to wrap her arms across her breasts or hide her flat belly—as if to protect the precious new life nestled there.

As though sensing her chaotic thoughts, Luke turned his head and their eyes met, his mouth kicking up at one corner in a wicked half-smile that made her breathless. Okay, he was hot but that didn't mean she was 'in love' with him.

Besides, that would make her an idiot and…

and suddenly the room disappeared and it was just the two of them. Lilah felt as though she was suspended in simmering heat waves of sensation. Blood drained from her head and she thought, *Holy cow, it's... Dammit, this is a nightmare.*

He must have suspected something was up because he frowned and without taking his eyes from hers broke away from the group to head in their direction. Through the buzzing noise in her ears she heard Angie say, "Yep, she's got it bad, all right." She turned to Lilah. "So tell me again what happened in the mountains?"

Lilah stared wide-eyed at the blatant intent on Luke's face and gave a strangled sound of distress. There was no way she could pretend she wasn't having an emotional meltdown. Not with everyone watching and listening like she was the new hospital soap opera. She'd either burst into tears or laugh hysterically and blurt out the truth.

And, really, she couldn't face him right now. Not with this HUGE secret she was hiding.

So Lilah did the only rational thing she could think of. Shoving back from the table, she lurched to her feet and with a strangled "Can't talk now," she bolted from the room, conscious of the shocked gazes following her retreat.

Luke watched Lilah blanch then turn rosy as a blush crept up her neck into her cheeks. He might have been concerned by the look of horror on her face if he wasn't instantly distracted by the memory of tracing that delicate tide of color with his lips. Just thinking about it made him a little crazy—as though she was a drug he'd suddenly become addicted to and couldn't be without. And when he remembered the unbelievably sexy sounds she made in the back of her throat, his body went hard and his lips curved in anticipation.

He'd never met a woman who was such a mass of suppressed simmering passion. And when he thought of the way she ignited in his arms, he discovered something about himself that made him a little uncomfortable. A very primitive need to be the only man to see those cool grey eyes turn all smoky an instant before her body caught fire. Because just the thought of her with someone else made him want to hit something.

But those were dangerous thoughts. He'd watched his parents' marriages implode and had decided a long time ago that he wasn't hardwired for love and marriage. Besides, the last thing his children needed was the Sullivan brand of marital hell he and his brothers had endured.

Realizing the direction of his thoughts, Luke snorted. Since when was he thinking about marriage and kids? He had no intention of having either. He'd clearly lost his mind and it was all Lilah's fault.

The other night after his heart rate had slowed he'd caught her watching him with solemn grey eyes. And when he'd asked if something was wrong she'd told him she didn't want him to worry about her getting any ideas.

*Ideas? What the hell?*

Blissfully unaware of his stunned confusion, she'd hurriedly assured him that as far as she was concerned they were just having a temporary fling because she needed to concentrate on getting her life in order. *In order for what?* Besides, he was leaving soon, she'd said, and she was okay with them just messing around until then.

*Okay? Messing around? Again, what the hell?*

He'd felt a little insulted that so soon after making her eyes roll back in her head she was telling him he was a messy distraction. Instead of being happy—because he sure as hell didn't want anything more than a hot fling—he'd been annoyed because he'd suddenly realized that he wasn't ready to move on. And he certainly wasn't ready for Lilah to move on.

But something was obviously wrong, he thought with a frown, because she was acting weird. Maybe she was having second thoughts about them. Maybe she'd been trying to tell him that she'd met someone else and was letting him down easy.

*Easy? Hell.* Luke's gut clenched at the thought,

and with narrow-eyed determination he headed across the room.

He must have looked a little fierce because Lilah's eyes widened and she shoved back from the table and scrambled for the exit.

Not about to let her escape, he followed, determined to get to the bottom of her weird behavior.

He found her slumped against the wall beside the elevators, hands over her face and muttering like she was casting a spell—or talking to herself.

He said casually, "Hey, what's up?" and chuckled when she squeaked and lurched upright like he'd zapped her. He wanted to know what the hell she'd been thinking about to put that look of horrified guilt on her face.

"I'd give anything to know what you're thinking right now," he drawled, propping his shoulder against the wall and folding his arms across his chest.

Lilah shook her head, looking adorably flustered—and nervous. Nervous?

"No, you wouldn't," she said, blowing irritably at a tendril of hair. He reached out a hand to tuck the silky strands behind her ear and smiled smugly when his touch made her shiver.

"How do you know I wouldn't?"

She rolled her eyes and scuttled backwards. "Because I'm thinking about how cute babies are even when they're upchucking on you."

"Cute?" he snorted, grinning when he spied some unidentified stains on her scrub top that he assumed was baby upchuck. "There's nothing cute about infant projectile vomiting and even less about it coming out the other end."

Lilah grimaced and shoved him away. "They're not always doing that."

He snorted again. "Right, other times they're screaming loud enough to strip paint off the walls."

Lilah's heart sank. "You really hate kids, don't you?"

Luke ruffled her hair like she was twelve. "Nah. Kids are okay." Her heart lifted hopefully and she managed a smile that faded at his next words. "As long as they're someone else's." He shook his head. "But not for me. I'm not father material."

"How do you know that?" Lilah demanded, and the look on Luke's face sent her spirits plummeting. Dammit, she was getting whiplash with all these wildly swinging emotions.

"I just do," Luke drawled, folding his arms across his chest. "We're products of our upbringing and whether we like it or not history tends to repeat itself." *No kidding*, Lilah thought with a touch of hysteria. "I have absolutely no intention of inflicting my childhood on an innocent kid."

"Who said you would? I mean, you're not your father."

"I know myself," he said with a finality that had tears stinging the backs of her eyes. Reaching out, he brushed a knuckle along her jaw. "Hey, what's up? You seem…I don't know. Sad. Nervous. And you're pale. Is something wrong? Are you still sick?" he asked gently, just as the doors opened to reveal a few department heads with their briefcases.

Peter Webster smiled when he spotted Lilah. Ignoring Luke, he pressed the button to hold the doors open. "You coming, Dr. Meredith?"

Hugely relieved at the offer of escape, she smiled back. "Yes," she said at the same time Luke said, "No," effortlessly preventing her from stepping into the elevator. He even pulled her close in an uncharacteristically possessive move. "We'll take the next one."

When the doors finally closed, Lilah demanded, "What are you doing?" and shoved away from him to retreat a few paces. The only way she could say what needed to be said was to be far away from the temptation to cling and maybe even beg a little. Because this whole disaster had made her realize one important, irrefutable fact. Her feelings for Luke Sullivan were in no way casual. And despite her insistence they were having nothing more than a fling, the joke was clearly on her. What she felt for him was as casual as an outbreak of hemorrhagic fever.

Distressed by the unwelcome realization, she wrapped her arms around herself. "Listen, Luke," she began hoarsely. "I um…I think we need to um…talk."

"Uh-oh," he said, narrowing his eyes on her. "I think I know where this is going?"

Lilah's pulse leapt with alarm. How could he know when she'd just found out this morning?

"You…do?"

"It's okay, Lilah," he sighed, irritably shoving an impatient hand through his hair. "I get it. I got it the first time you brought it up and I totally agree."

Lilah frowned with confusion. Brought what up? What was he talking about? "You do?" she asked again, starting to sound like a parrot.

"Yep. You're not into anything serious with me and you want to keep it light. I get it." He shrugged as if it didn't matter but his jaw was hard and his eyes unreadable. "Besides, I just got out of the military and the last thing…the very last thing I want is more responsibility or a serious relationship."

Lilah swallowed past the hot tears clogging her throat. "It is?"

"Yep," he said again. "The Sullivan boys aren't into relationships and I'm enjoying what we have now. I don't suppose I have to tell you that." He lifted a hand and brushed his thumb over her lips, grinning wickedly when she gasped and backed up a step. His gaze heated at the way she licked her lips. "And I know you're having a great time too," he murmured roughly, clearly thinking about how great a time she'd had last night and then again this morning.

Lilah blushed, tempted to slide into his seductive green gaze and forget everything but the way he made her feel. But she would still be pregnant and he would still be against having children. "I did…I mean I am, but the thing is…" She paused and drew in a shaky breath. "Things, um, change and I—" Suddenly they heard voices and Lilah panicked. "I have to go."

"Not so fast," Luke growled, wrapping his big hand around her arm and guiding her towards the emergency exit. "You're not running away now."

"Wha—? No," she said, but Luke tugged her through the door. "I'm not running." *Much.* "I just can't have this conversation now, that's all."

"What conversation is that?" he demanded, his back to the stairwell door, as though to prevent her escape.

Lilah flushed and nervously smoothed her hair off her face, wondering if she could beat him down the stairs. "Well, that I…um…that I can't afford to mess up. Not again. And especially not now."

"Again?" He sighed. "I told you it wasn't your fault."

Her mouth dropped open. "You did?"

"You're not responsible for other people's actions," he said with gentle insistence. "Your father doesn't deserve you and that moron ex-boss should be arrested. Stop punishing yourself."

"Oh, that."

Luke frowned at her lack of enthusiasm. "What did you think I meant?"

Lilah drew in a shaky breath and blinked back tears. She couldn't do this now. Maybe not ever.

"Nothing. It doesn't matter. I just don't think we should see each other again...I mean, with my career and you..." She petered out at the look on his face.

"And me what?" he demanded, looking a little insulted.

"Well, you're...leaving," she said lamely.

"Yes, but not right now." Luke shoved his hands on his hips. "What the hell is this about, Lilah? I thought this was what you wanted. A good time with no strings."

She licked her lips nervously and couldn't stop a flood of tears obscuring her vision. She wrapped her arms around her body and her gaze slid away guiltily as she drew in a shaky breath. "The thing is..." She gulped.

In the loaded silence Luke finished her sentence for her with, "You've met someone else?"

Lilah was too shocked to say anything other than, "*Wha-at*?"

"That's it, isn't it?" he growled, and then next instant he pushed her against the stairwell wall, and pinning her hands above her head, pressed his body against hers. "So who is it? Webster?" Lilah lifted her head to stare into his furious green eyes. The automatic denial that rose to her lips died.

Misinterpreting her silence, Luke snarled and pushed closer.

"Fine, then."

"What are you doing?" she squeaked breathlessly, and froze when she felt his hardness against her belly. He was angry and aroused; a combination that made her pulse leap and her blood heat.

"Let's call this a farewell kiss, then, shall we?" he ground out furiously, and lowered his head, crushing her mouth with his and stifling Lilah's gasp.

The kiss instantly spiraled out of control and she was helpless against the onslaught. For several seconds she tried to block out the feelings he aroused in her, but she'd never been successful at ignoring him or the way he made her feel. With a ragged moan she slid her hands up his chest and melted against him.

As though her surrender was the sign he'd been waiting for, Luke abruptly released her wrists and shoved away from her.

"Webster? Seriously?" he panted, looking sav-

agely pleased when she sagged against the wall
and stared at him through passion-dazed eyes.
"He'll toss you aside faster than a used movie
ticket. Is that what you want?"

And when she continued to stare at him he
cursed and turned away, ripping open the stairwell door before flinging one last parting shot
over his shoulder. "*Fine*. Just…stay out of trou-,
ble," he grated hoarsely, before disappearing.

Lilah gaped at the closing door, vaguely conscious that she was breathing heavily and that
her body felt boneless. It was all she could do to
remain propped against the wall. After a couple
of beats she lifted a shaky hand to her bruised
lips and thought, *Holy bejeezers. What the heck
just happened?*

And why did it make her feel as though her
heart was being ripped from her chest? And why
was she shivering, hugging herself and crying
about the emptiness left behind?

Shoving her fist in her bruised mouth to stifle
the sobs, Lilah heard the echo of his final snarled
words. *Stay out of trouble?* A hysterical laugh
caught in her throat. Oh, boy. That was rich, considering she'd landed herself in a huge heap of it.

And he thought she'd met someone else. Could
*be* with anyone else after being with him. Dammit, didn't he know he was like a level-five tornado, sucking up everything in his path? Her
bones, her breath…her mind. And she'd need all

three if she was going to do this alone because one thing was certain: the Meredith women were idiots when it came to men.

Sighing, Lilah banged her head against the wall as though the move would shake loose the memory of his eyes blazing with wounded anger. Although that was probably just his pride, she thought, because he'd never once hinted that he felt anything for her other than lust.

And she couldn't stay knowing it would fizzle out just as quickly as it had exploded. She couldn't do that to him or her…their child.

Finally Lilah pushed away from the wall. And feeling more alone than she'd ever felt in her life, she headed down the stairs on heavy, shaky legs.

*She really was on her own.*

# CHAPTER TWELVE

LUKE IGNORED THE people scurrying out of his way and headed for the ER like a man on a mission. At four o'clock this morning he'd gone jogging to clear his head and unclench his gut from the ball of tension that had taken up permanent residence there since he'd left Lilah slumped against the wall in the stairwell, tears swimming in her silvery eyes.

God, the memory of her devastated expression made him feel like a class-A bastard. And after replaying their conversation a million times in his head, he realized that he'd allowed his screwed-up childhood to blind him to the truth. A truth he'd ignored simply because the jumble of confusing emotions Lilah roused in him scared the hell out of him.

He'd looked into her eyes and felt his chest tighten with something he'd never felt before. He'd wanted to crush her close and never let go. He'd wanted to fight all her demons and protect her when he'd never felt the urge before. He'd also wanted to run. Far and fast.

And then she'd sprouted all that garbage about needing to focus on her career and he'd jumped to stupid conclusions, kissing her like he wanted to swallow her whole—before storming away like a rejected adolescent. And later, when he'd seen her with Webster, he'd gone a little crazy because, despite everything, the damn woman had burrowed beneath his skin and wormed her way into his heart.

And now that he was ready to listen, she wouldn't talk. In fact, she'd gone AWOL and no one knew where she was. Or they weren't talking. Especially not to him. But, *dammit*, he missed her. Missed her smile and the way she made him feel—even when he didn't want to acknowledge it—like he'd finally come home.

And he'd honestly thought she was starting to feel the same way. Until she'd blindsided him with the "I don't think we should see each other" speech. But now, recalling the look of misery on her face, he had to wonder if something else wasn't wrong. Like someone harassing her— threatening to have her fired if she didn't play their sick game. Someone like Webster.

Luke growled low in his throat and vowed retribution if he found out the guy was up to his old tricks with her. As an army ranger he knew a hundred ways to get a man to spill his guts.

And he'd use every one of them on the slime-ball and enjoy it.

Pausing before the ER doors, Luke pulled out his phone and checked in case Lilah had returned his calls. She hadn't. And he was really starting to worry. Especially since no one knew where she was other than she'd taken a couple of sick days.

He'd tried calling her last night but she hadn't answered and eventually his calls had gone straight to voicemail. So he'd gone to her house but it had been in darkness and she hadn't answered when he'd pounded on the door. If her neighbor hadn't stuck her head out an upstairs window and threatened to call the cops, Luke would have spent the night on her porch—or broken into her house, tied her to the bed and forced the truth from her.

He'd returned home only to head out again at four for a run to clear his head because he hadn't been able to sleep and was clearly a basket case. He was beginning to feel like a stalker. He was beginning to feel that old sense of impending doom. Only this time because he was imagining all kinds of disasters, the worst being that she needed him and he wasn't there.

Thrusting the phone into his pocket, he slammed the doors open with the heel of his hand and ignored the startled looks of people hastily scrambling out of his way as he stomped across the ER waiting room.

He was an army ranger, for God's sake. And considering rangers could find a lone camel in the desert, he could damn well find one annoying woman who thought she could hide from him.

He caught sight of Lilah's friend, Angie Something-or-other, and changed direction, prepared to torture Lilah's whereabouts from her if he had to.

"Where is she?" he growled in lieu of a greeting, and after her initial surprise the woman folded her arms across her chest and looked at him like he was something to be scraped off the bottom of her shoe.

"Why do you care?" she demanded, the hard glint in her narrowed eyes indicating that her mood was as dangerous as his. But Luke didn't have time to feel insulted or explain. He was trying to ignore the growing feeling of urgency.

"Of course I care," he spluttered, straightening to his full height and mirroring her pose. But the woman obviously didn't know a desperate man when she saw one.

"Oh, right," she snapped. "That's why you accused her of sleeping around and dumped her faster than last year's tinned beans when you found out about the baby. Great way to show you care, dumb-ass."

"I didn't accuse her cheating," he said a little defensively. "I was—" He broke off to frown as something she'd said suddenly registered. "Whoa, back up there, sister. Baby? What baby?"

"Nothing. Forget I said anything."

"Oh, no, you don't," he said, grabbing her arm when she made to walk away. "What the hell are you talking about?"

Angie rolled her eyes. "Why do you think she's been so tired and sick lately?"

Luke stared at her, his mind racing. "She told me it was stress."

Angie snorted derisively. "And you call yourself a doctor. She's about eight weeks pregnant, Sullivan." Luke opened his mouth to say that it was impossible because they'd always used a condom, but before he could get anything out Angie moved closer and growled furiously. "And if you say it's not yours, I'll break your nose."

"Wha—?" He paused and shoved shaking fingers through his hair when he remembered the one time they hadn't used protection. *Oh, man*, eight weeks was about right. "Why didn't she tell me?"

"She tried but you kept going on about leaving and being just like your father, blah, blah, blah. Like you haven't got the guts to be your own man." She glared at him as though daring him to deny it. "And because she thinks it's déjà vu all over again. Only this time it's not her father rejecting her but some rich playboy doctor enjoying... His. Latest. Fling." She punctuated each snarled word with a jab of her finger in his chest.

Luke retreated under the attack and stared at Angie as though she'd stuck a knife between his ribs. Hell, she might as well have stabbed him in the heart. "Wha-at? She said that?"

"She thinks she's not good enough for someone like you," Angie snapped.

"That's ridiculous," Luke growled, and shoved a hand through his hair again with mounting frustration. "I never said that. I *would* never say that. Besides, I joined the army to get away from that kind of life and I have no intention of going back to it." He growled. "It's me, not her."

Angie rolled her eyes and growled low in her throat. "That's the oldest line in the book, you jackass."

Luke opened his mouth to object when he realized she was right. He shut it with a snap, his lips twisting into a derisive smile. He was a jackass and he only had to really look at himself to see that he was nothing like his father.

Thinking he found the situation amusing, Angie punched him. "You arrogant jerk, she and the baby are better off without you."

Luke's amusement faded and his gut turned to stone when he recalled the last expression he'd seen on Lilah's face. Did she really think he wouldn't want her…or the baby they'd made together? Did she really think he was just like his father? Or worse. Hers? "How could she not tell me?" he demanded, but he knew. She'd talked about how cute babies were and he'd reacted negatively.

"You're a smart guy," Angie snorted, but her tone indicated otherwise. "Figure it out. But know one thing, you bastard," she said, suddenly fiercely angry. "If anything happens to her or the baby, I'll kill you myself."

Taken aback by her vehemence, Luke felt the blood drain from his head and wondered if he was going crazy. "Happens to her? What do you mean? Where is she?" He was practically yelling by the time he finished and people were staring, but he didn't care. He grabbed Angie's shoulders and shook her. "Tell me," he snarled, and for a moment the woman stared at him as though he was a crazy person. Hell, he felt crazy—and scared.

"She took a flight call."

*"Wha-at?"* Luke reared back and gaped at her as his mind raced. *Dammit*, he'd pulled strings to get her off the flight list because he'd known she was still having nightmares.

Hell, *he* was still having nightmares…and flashbacks.

She'd all but fallen out of the mangled chopper and promptly tossed her cookies. She'd been injured and had suffered a mild concussion, and he winced when he remembered the extent of her bruising. How could she do that again? Especially as another storm was moving in from the coast. Especially in her condition?

Luke swore viciously and swung away, feeling the need to punch something—anything.

"I told her not to go," Angie gulped, glaring at him as though he was responsible. "But she wouldn't listen and it's your fault."

Shoving both hands in his hair, Luke fought the feeling of helplessness that gripped him and he experienced gut-wrenching fear for perhaps the first time in his life.

"Who the hell ordered it?" he yelled. "I made sure she was taken off the damn—"

"What the *hell* is going on?" an authoritative voice snapped out behind them, and Luke spun around, fiercely glad of a target deserving of his fury. "You're causing a scene," Webster accused impatiently, before Luke could rip him a new one. "Get back to work, Prescott. Sullivan, aren't you supposed to be off rotation? Because if you can't stay away, I suggest you put on some scrubs and take room four. With Dr. Meredith out on flight call we're short-staffed."

Ignoring Webster's question, which was probably rhetorical anyway, Luke demanded, "Who the hell authorized that flight?" His menacing tone froze the other man in his tracks.

Webster blinked. "I did," he admitted, looking a little wary in the face of Luke's hostility. "But she insisted," he added quickly, when Luke's expression turned murderous. "In fact, she said if I didn't let her go she w-would report me for harassment."

Luke narrowed his eyes. "You're lying."

"I'm not," he denied hotly. "I swear. You can even ask my secretary." He gulped, his eyes widening in his suddenly pale face. "She'll confirm it."

Luke's expression turned grim as fear clenched his gut. "Where did they go and how long have they been gone?" he demanded, his voice tight with fury.

Webster fidgeted nervously before confessing, "Copper Canyon, and they've only been gone a few hours. We lost contact a little while ago but—"

Luke drew back his arm and planted his fist in the smarmy bastard's well-moisturized face. Webster's head snapped back and there was a collective gasp as he staggered and fell. Everyone who'd gathered to watch the scene taking place froze. No one moved to help the head of ER and after a few stunned moments Peter shook his head and blinked up at Luke like he was struggling to focus.

"What the hell was that for?" he gasped, lifting his hand to the blood pouring from his broken nose.

"That's for sending her out with a storm brewing," Luke snarled like an avenging angel. "That's for putting your hands on her, and daring to breathe in her direction." He bent close, seething with fury and fear. "And if you ever go near her again, I'll—"

"Sullivan!"

Luke turned to glare at Greg Turner hurrying towards them, white-faced and urgent.

"Don't try and stop me, Turner," he snarled. "Someone has to teach this piece of—"

"It's Lilah," Greg gulped, barely giving the man on the floor a second glance. "We just got word. The chopper went down in the storm." He gulped and looked as though he was about to cry. "Man, I'm sorry, buddy. It crashed. The chopper crashed in the mountains."

# CHAPTER THIRTEEN

THE NEXT FEW hours were possibly the worst Luke had ever endured. For the first time in his life he was afraid—more afraid than he'd been during the fourteen hours he'd held off enemy forces. More afraid than when his helicopter had been shot down by an RPG and he had been trapped with the dead and dying, wondering if he was going to die himself.

Now all he could think about was Lilah out there somewhere, alone and injured, thinking that she was destined to die in a crash, just like her mother. Thinking he didn't care about her... or their baby.

They needed him and he wasn't going to fail them. Not again.

With that thought uppermost, Luke weaseled—okay, threatened—their last known location from the despatcher and tore through the pouring rain to the nearest airfield. If he couldn't find anyone to fly him in this weather, he would take a chopper, fly it into the mountains himself and face the consequences later.

With the rain making a puddle around him, he whipped out his gold credit card and the keys to his bike and shoved them across the counter. "I need the chopper out front."

"What?" The woman behind the counter gaped at him, probably because he looked a little crazy. "But...but...the storm," she stuttered nervously. "It's too dangerous to fly in that."

"It's an emergency," he snapped, and without waiting headed around the counter towards the large board holding a variety of keys. "I'll pay whatever you want. I'll even buy the damn chopper. Just give me the damn keys."

"Sir, you need to sign papers...a waiver? If you wait a moment I'll call the owner."

"Call the police," Luke informed her curtly. "Call the damn National Guard. I need that chopper now. Which keys?"

"Sir—"

"It's a matter of life and death," Luke interrupted impatiently. "Do you want to be responsible for someone's death?"

The woman paled beneath his challenging stare, her eyes going huge. "I...uh...I'm not sure..."

"I didn't think so. Look, the woman I...I..." Luke paused and felt the earth shift beneath his feet as the truth dawned. He slapped the side of his head and thought, *Of course!* Of course he loved her. He loved her smile, the way she gasped his name when she came; he loved her laugh and the way she got all clumsy when she was flustered.

*God*, he missed her more than he'd thought possible. And he needed her in his life even though he'd told himself he didn't need anyone. It was the reason he'd reacted so badly when in the past he wouldn't have cared if the woman he was with had found someone else. It was the reason he was frantic to find her, keep her safe.

Keep them both safe.

*Dammit.* If anything had happened to her... *No.* He shook his head decisively. He couldn't... *wouldn't* lose her. Not now that he'd found her. Not now that he realized he needed her as much if not more than she needed him...because if something happened to her he didn't think he would ever recover from the loss.

But he needed to get a grip, and fast. She needed him thinking clearly, not panicking like a rookie. And he wasn't going to fail her. Not if he could help it. Not like everyone else in her life.

"The woman I...love is out there somewhere," he said, feeling a little shell-shocked by his discovery and the realization that she was in serious trouble. "She's a doctor on a flight emergency when her chopper went down."

"It's really too dangerous out there," she was

saying gently, as though placating an escapee from the psych ward, but Luke barely heard her through the pounding in his head.

*Dammit*, he was wasting time. "I'm sorry but I'm taking that chopper with or without your permission. I need—"

"Fine," the woman interrupted, and turned to snag a set of keys from the board, which she tossed at him. "Here. Go." She waved him away, calling out, "You'd better bring it back in one piece or I'm calling the police," as he ran into the rain.

Lilah drifted in and out of consciousness, vaguely aware that despite being icy cold and wet, fire engulfed her entire right side. She'd tried moving away from the pain but every time she did it intensified.

Her head felt like someone had split it open with a baseball bat and with every breath nausea swam around in her stomach, threatening a major revolt.

At some point she heard an annoying buzzing sound that roused her but when she strained to listen for it, all she heard was the rain. Oh, and someone groaning. She was pretty sure it wasn't her.

She also thought she heard Luke calling her but when she tried to focus her head hurt so much she wept. Exhausted by her efforts, she let herself be drawn back into the beckoning darkness, only to jolt awake when something brushed her cheek.

Thinking it was a wild animal, Lilah cried out and tried to shift away, but the move sent pain roaring through her like a firestorm while somewhere close she heard a voice calling.

"Lilah." It must be an angel, she decided, because the sound filled her with a sense of peace, drawing her upwards toward the light.

"Lilah, open your eyes, babe. I've got you."

She opened her mouth to tell the angel that she didn't think she should go with him because then her baby would be alone.

Luke would also be alone and she knew instinctively that he needed her. She wished he was there.

His name emerged on a ragged sigh. "Luke."

"I'm here, sweetheart. I'm here. Why don't you open your eyes and see for yourself? No, don't close them," he murmured soothingly, when she blinked and her eyelids involuntarily drifted shut, despite her best efforts to keep them open.

"That's it, darlin'…just a little more." Lilah blinked his face into focus. "There's my beautiful wild woman." Gentle fingers smoothed her hair off her face. "Tell me where it hurts."

Lilah struggled to focus on the words but they kept getting louder then softer and she couldn't see out of her right eye no matter how many times she blinked.

"It hurts," she whispered, her gaze clinging to his fuzzy outline.

"What does?"

"My…my head. Why can't I see?"

"Don't panic, you hit your head and there's a small laceration." His bulk loomed closer and his fingers moved gently through her hair, probing and soothing. She let out a moan when he hit a particularly tender spot and thought he might have kissed her but wasn't sure. Her forehead wrinkled in confusion and she struggled to make sense of what was happening.

"What…what happened?"

"There was a little accident, sweetheart," he murmured, gently smoothing away the stress between her brows. "But you're going to be fine now. I promise."

Lilah tried shifting to relieve the pressure against her side, and ended up breathing through the pain. "Luke…"

"Yeah?"

"I think…I think the chopper crashed," she rasped heavily. "How bad is it? Where's Jerry? I think I heard him moaning." He moved away briefly, returning to brush his knuckles against her cheek when she cried out.

"I'm just going to move this piece of metal," he promised soothingly. "I'm right here."

Lilah sucked in a breath, moaning when something shifted and pain swept through her like a fiery explosion. "Stop. *Stop*!"

"Hey. *Hey*." Luke gentled her with a large hand on her uninjured shoulder, smoothing a path to her hand and back again. "I've got to get you out of here, babe, and to do that I have to move you. You trust me, don't you?"

Tears blurred her vision and a sudden thought had her gripping him. "The baby," she said fiercely. "Please tell me the baby is okay!" She broke off on a sob, vaguely aware of hot tears streaming down her face to mingle with cold rain.

"Relax, sweetheart," Luke murmured comfortingly, but Lilah wondered at the hoarseness in his voice. She struggled to see his expression, but it was dark and she couldn't seem to focus.

"Luke—?"

"I'm not going to let anything happen to the baby," he promised fiercely, brushing trembling fingers over her lips. Or was she the one shaking? She didn't know. Only that she was cold and his hands were warm. "But I need to move you and I want you to focus on me, on my eyes. Can you do that for me?"

She blinked up at him and sent him a crooked smile. Of course she could. His eyes were a beautiful green, so full of fierce emotion, and she loved looking into them…loved him.

His gaze caught and held hers, intense and serious and…yet…there was something else there as well. Something she couldn't recognize through the haze of pain. Something that filled her with strength and a warm, hopeful glow. But she needed to tell him something…something important.

"Luke…"

"I've got you. If you believe nothing else, babe. Believe that."

With her eyes locked on his Lilah opened her mouth to reassure him and "Don't let me go," emerged on a strangled sob. The last thing she saw was Luke's fervent expression and heard his equally fervent assurance.

"I don't intend to." His fierce murmur faded into the distance, and just before the darkness claimed her she thought he said, "I love you too much to let go ever again."

Lilah became aware of an irritating beeping noise that sounded vaguely familiar and filled her with an urgency she didn't understand. Finally forcing her eyes open, she took in the shadowed room and the familiar sight of hospital equipment.

*What the…?*

Confused, she lifted a hand to her face and gasped when the move sent sharp pain radiating through her body. Almost instantly a large hand engulfed hers in warm comfort.

"I'm here," a deep comforting voice murmured from the shadows. "Try not to move."

"Where—?"

"You're safe," he said. "Just rest."

Lilah instantly quieted, the firm touch filling her with a strange lassitude and a welcome sense of security.

The voice sounded too emotional to be Luke, she thought woozily, and rasped, "Water," into the silence.

A straw lightly touched her lips and she latched onto it, drinking greedily before the effort exhausted her. She felt her eyelids flutter closed and the hand was back, soothing and gentle as she slid towards sleep.

"Luke."

"I'm here," he crooned. "Everything's going to be just fine." And just before darkness claimed her she thought she heard him say, "I love you, Wild Woman. I'm here. I'll be here when you wake. I promise," and wondered who he was talking to.

The next time Lilah drifted awake it was quiet. The kind of quiet that told her she was alone. Sunlight streamed through the windows and lit up the small room, making it bright and somehow optimistic.

For a few minutes she floated on a cloud of

lassitude enjoying the rare opportunity to sleep in. Between one breath and the next memory returned and the warm glow she'd woken with popped.

Her eyes flew open and a quick look around the empty room confirmed her suspicions. She'd survived a chopper crash and was alone in a hospital room. Clearly whatever she'd thought had happened after that had been a dream.

A nice dream…but a dream nonetheless, because in her dream he'd promised to be here. And he wasn't. But, then, she wasn't really surprised since he was probably long go—

"Hey. What's with the gloomy face?"

A storm of conflicting emotions assailed Lilah at the sound of that deep, rough voice. Disbelief, joy, anger, betrayal…and an overwhelming sense of relief. Turning, she caught sight of him in the doorway looking tired and rumpled and just…*wonderful*. Her breath caught at the familiar sight of his amazing green eyes, burning with an expression that made hers fill with tears.

"What's wrong?" he demanded urgently, when she stared silently up at him through swimming eyes. "Are you in pain?"

Lilah bit her lip and shook her head. She wanted to be mad at him but couldn't drum up the energy. Maybe because he looked exhausted and worried…and deliciously rumpled. Maybe because all that emotion was aimed at her.

"You look terrible."

A smile tugged at one corner of his tight mouth and amusement briefly lit his shadowed eyes. "And you look like you got between a chopper and a mountain," he replied, placing his fingers gently against her inner wrist to check her pulse. She didn't know why he bothered as she was hooked up to the machine which was still beeping annoyingly.

"I dreamed a huge eagle rescued me and flew me up into the mountains."

That almost-smile flashed as his eyes studied her intently. "You did, huh?"

"I thought…I thought maybe I was dreaming. I remember the rotors spraying up rocks and branches." She gulped. "I had my eyes squeezed shut, praying really hard, and the next thing—"

"Don't think about it," Luke urged gently, and leaned closer to peer into her eyes. Apparently satisfied by whatever he saw there, he straightened, sliding his hand down to link his fingers with hers and giving them a gentle squeeze.

Lilah gulped at the tender gesture and wondered if she was high on morphine or if he'd lost his mind.

She slid her free hand down to her belly. "The baby—?"

"Is fine," he said, his voice hoarse with an emotion she couldn't quite identify. He swallowed visibly. "You're both fine. Or you will be."

"Promise?"

"You injured your side, but the baby is absolutely okay."

Oh, thank God, she thought with relief, but said instead, "I heard you calling me. It was annoying and woke me up."

His eyes twinkled. "Annoying, huh?"

"I guess it saved me," she admitted grudgingly, and he lifted her hand to his lips, his eyes shimmering over the top of her knuckles as though he was struggling to hold onto his control.

"Why didn't you tell me?" he demanded gently, giving her a little nip and sending delight winging through the pain. "About the baby, I mean."

Lilah's heart clenched and she averted her eyes, tugging her hand free. He might know about the baby but that didn't mean he wanted to be part of their life.

Her own father hadn't.

"I…couldn't," she whispered through a throat tight with tears. "Not when you were so…adamant." She shook her head. "I don't want my child to feel like a mistake."

His eyes flared before he caught at her hand and engulfed it in heat. "Never," she barely heard him say. "Never a mistake, Lilah. How could it be?"

Shock made her speechless. "Wh-at?" she

croaked. Okay, almost speechless, but, *damn*… she was getting more confused by the second. Maybe the head injury was more serious than she'd thought.

A dull red rose up his throat and he looked a little abashed. "Not when this baby has someone like you for a mother. They're going to be the luckiest kid alive."

Lilah stared at him for several beats. "What… what about his father?"

"His? What if it's a girl? Because I want a little girl with long sunset-colored curls and big grey eyes."

"What about her father, then?" she whispered, her eyes solemn. "Will he be the luckiest man?"

"Maybe…maybe she doesn't want someone like me to be her father," he admitted quietly, his eyes locked on their hands, as though he couldn't bear for her to see the emotions he was struggling with. "Besides, I broke more than a few traffic laws and stole a chopper so I might get arrested. No little girl deserves a jailbird as a father."

"What?"

He looked up and sent her a crooked smile. "I went a little crazy when I heard you went out on the flight call. *Dammit*, I fixed it so you wouldn't have to go again. Why did you?

Lilah stared at him open-mouthed. "I, uh…"

"And then we heard you crashed and I kind

of lost it—*Jeez.*" He took a deep breath and his fingers tightened on hers.

"Lost it? Crazy?"

He dropped his forehead onto their joined hands and gave a rough snort before lifting his head to grin. "Everyone is calling me Looney Luke."

"Are you? Crazy, I mean."

"Yep," he said, sending her a stern glance. "And it's your fault."

"Me?" Lilah she was having trouble following the conversation, especially as she was trying to interpret the expression in his eyes at the same time. It made her belly clench, her chest tighten and her head a little dizzy, like she'd swallowed too much helium. But it could also be from concussion. "You're not making any sense."

His mouth twisted into a crooked grin. "I threatened your best friend and punched out your boss."

"Who—Angie?"

"I couldn't find you," he accused. "And you weren't answering your cell. So I acted like a crazy person. It's a miracle they didn't call the cops. Or send Security over to lock me in the psych ward."

A smile bloomed over Lilah's face. "You punched out Webster?"

"It would have been more satisfying if he hadn't gone down like a wimp."

"My hero."

His amusement faded. "No," he said, his expression somber. "I'm no hero, Lilah. I'm just a man." He shook his head and gave a broken laugh. "A man who loves you more than he thought possible. A man who almost lost the best thing that could ever happen to him." He drew in a sharp breath, as though trying to control his emotions. "But I've got you now," he told her fiercely. "Both of you. And I'm going to spend the rest of my life holding on."

"The rest…?"

"But you have to promise never to scare me like that again. In fact, I insist on it."

"You…do?"

"Yep, but I somehow don't think it's going to be a problem."

Lilah frowned at the laughter lighting his green eyes and wondered what he was up to.

"How can you know that?" she demanded, shivering at the way his lips brushed across the top of her knuckles.

"You do realize that you've crashed in two helicopters in the last two months, don't you? Well," he said without waiting for a reply, "no one's willing to bet on those odds and they're signing a petition to have you removed from the roster. They say you're jinxed."

Lilah's eyes widened. "Wha-at?"

Luke snorted. "In fact, since we've both survived two crashes we're both jinxed."

"Jinxed? But that's ridiculous. Do people really believe in that stuff?"

"And since we're jinxed they're saying we deserve each other." His gaze lost its twinkle and turned serious. "That we clearly belong together," he concluded softly, and Lilah sucked in a sharp breath at his fierce expression.

"Together?"

"Uh-huh. They're calling us Looney Luke and Wild Woman." He chuckled and shook his head. "Like we're some kind of disaster duo comicbook heroes."

"And you, Luke? What do you think?"

His smile became tender and fierce emotion shimmered in his eyes. "Well, I definitely don't deserve you but I think our baby is going to be the luckiest kid alive."

"Because we're the disaster duo?"

"No," he murmured, leaning down to cover her mouth with his. "Because." *Kiss*. "Her mother." *Another kiss*. "Loves her father." *Yet another kiss*. "And her father…" Another kiss, this one lingering for long breathless beats until he broke off to suck in a ragged breath. He stared into her eyes as he struggled with words and some fierce emotions.

"And her father…?" Lilah prompted, just as breathlessly.

"And her father can't live without her mother."

Lilah's breath hitched. "What are you saying, Luke?"

Staring into her eyes, he said quietly, clearly, "I'm saying I love you."

Lilah gasped. That she was shocked by his confession was an understatement and all she could say was, "But you…you don't want a relationship. Or a family."

He grimaced and looked down to where his thumb was caressing the back of her hand. "I know I said that, but I do. As long as it's with you. No, *only* if it's with you."

"What…?" Lilah searched his expression. "What about your plans to leave Washington?"

"Plans change."

"Is this about the baby, Luke?" she asked quietly, tugging at her hand, which he refused to relinquish. "Because if it is—"

"It isn't," he interrupted. "At least, not entirely." He sighed and shoved a hand through his hair. "I love you, Lilah, and when I thought I might never get to see you again or tell you how I feel, I completely lost it. I want—no, I *need*—to be with you."

Lilah gulped and in a small voice said, "Oh."

"Oh?" Luke rose from the chair he'd pulled close to the bed and folded his arms across his wide chest to stare down at her. He was clearly a little steamed. "Is that all you can say? I spill my guts and all you say is 'Oh'?"

"I…I…" Lilah paused and gulped as the words trembled on her lips. Her breath escaped in a whoosh as she prepared to take the plunge. "I…love you too?"

For several beats he stared at her as though she'd admitted to stealing the crown jewels and then his eyes softened to something so warm and tender that tears blurred her vision.

"Finally," he murmured, and sank back into the chair. "I thought I might have to give up my left nut before I got to hear you say those words."

Lilah rolled her eyes. "Your…nuts are safe… for now," she told him with a watery smile. "As long as I get to keep the crazy guy they're attached to."

Luke grinned and turned his head to press a gentle kiss into her palm. "I'm yours, wild thing. Forever. Now it's your turn."

"My turn?" she teased, and when he nipped the fleshy part of her thumb she said on a delicious shiver, "I love you, Luke, as long as you're sure it's me you want and not just the baby."

"I want you," he growled impatiently, and protectively covered the hand placed over her belly. "You." He leaned forward to kiss her. "Although I'm happy about Wild Child Sullivan. Now… could you, Lilah Paige Meredith, marry someone like me? Could you love me forever and—?"

"Yes," she interrupted, her smile serene in the face of his obvious love and acceptance of their little miracle.

His beautifully sculpted mouth curled into a tender smirk. "Yes, what, wild thing?"

Tears filled Lilah's eyes. "Yes," she murmured, lifting her hand to cup his beard-roughened jaw, enjoying the rasp against her fingers. "We'll marry you, Looney Luke Sullivan. And we'll love you forever."

And with a fervently murmured "Thank you, God," the bad-boy army ranger bent and sealed their vow with a kiss.

* * * * *